AF244169

Neon Hemlock Press
www.neonhemlock.com
@neonhemlock

© 2025 T.T. Madden

The Cosmic Color
T..T. Madden

Cover and Interior Illustration by buttercup / btrcp.art
Cover Design and Interior Layout by dave ring
Edited by dave ring

Print ISBN-13: 978-1-952086-92-2
Ebook ISBN-13: 978-1-966503-02-6

T.T. Madden
THE COSMIC COLOR
Neon Hemlock Press

NEON HEMLOCK

THE
COSMIC
COLOR

BY T.T. MADDEN

For the Weirdos in the Wild,
who I told this story to before I ever wrote it down.

SOLANUM

PART I.

EGG

THE MACHINE'S COUNTDOWN hits zero, and Eric Fisher screams as a cosmic surge of energy runs through him. It's there and gone in an instant, just like the pain. And then everything else is gone too—all of his sensations, everything that connects him to the body he spent the last twenty-four years in. All gone. He's nothing but thoughts floating in an endless void.

This is the moment he's trained for, the moment he's dreamed of since he was a child.

Entering the mindscape is the next step in Eric's own personal fight back against the Imago, gargantuan, transformed creatures that have been ripping their way through the planet for the past several decades. Ever since he was a child, when he saw his very first pilot, the famous Darius Draven, he knew piloting was his destiny. Eric feared the monsters, of course, towering, reptilian things that were once human, horrifically transformed beyond saving.

But there was something beyond the fear, a calling that took hold of him when he saw Draven standing victoriously. He's been through boot camp, through the pilot exams, through simulator training, all to get to this place, the void all pilots experience before establishing the mental connection with their Instar, the enormous mechanical exosuits used to battle the Imago. It's an endless darkness, but not an uncomfortable one. It's an emptiness that includes only what Eric's mind brings to it, and in the flashes of light those harsh energies illuminate an image of Eric as a child, clutching action figures of famous Instars. He sees himself looking up at a recruitment poster of an Instar pointing at the viewer. He's training in his backyard, lifting weights, running sprints along the beach, waking up early in boot camp, taking pilot exams, hopping into the simulator, and he thinks of how he's finally here, finally where he wanted to be for so long. Eric knows this feeling won't last long, the void won't be like this forever, so he savors not having a body, existing only as his thoughts, as a mind, a soul. If that's, indeed, what he is at this moment. He's always wanted to believe people are more than a series of electrical signals, more complicated than a neocortex. That they are not just fleshy machines. But the truth of that is beyond him, will probably be beyond him forever, and he tries to find bliss in these few seconds he can be truly and utterly alone. For a moment, Eric Fisher is not a body, and a huge part of him is relieved at that. To feel the absence of corporeality.

Still, in this in-between place, it *appears* as if he has a body. He's been told the whole process is simpler that way, easier for the human mind to comprehend what's happening if it can at least arrange things in a way that makes sense. Eric has never told anyone he would prefer otherwise, that his mind doesn't need to fake it.

But it doesn't work like that. Inside this void, inside this machine, is as close as he's ever going to get to being ethereal.

Until death, he guesses.

Eric considers the void version of his body. It's nude, but he tries his best to ignore that, pushing his discomfort down and away. Staring at the void, looking sideways at a Black man's body lined with muscle and tattoos and scars. A body that has been through hell and will go through more over the next few years as an Instar pilot.

Yes, that is what he *sees*. But what he *feels* is a distance from his own physicality. Eric cannot explain, has never felt like he's had the words to tell, why his body is not just not his body, but something driven by something or someone else.

Eric swallows, mustering up a strength, before this phantom projection of him that still bears its scars. Their memories should hurt. And in a way they do. But with each scar he's been given, each tattoo etched into his skin, Eric makes his body more his own. Each marking not a marring, but a souvenir of an experience that belongs to him and him alone. Even if—especially if—those experiences were tough. Childhood fights. Boot camp. Instar training. With each one he came a little bit closer to himself and what he was meant to be. Or, perhaps, he's beginning to chip away at a new version of himself, uncovered from the block of granite he was given at the beginning of his life.

Electric lines of violet light crawl through the darkness. Eric is surprised the cosmic color reveals itself to him in bolts of lavender lightning; he thinks of violet, lavender, the family of purples, as feminine colors. But he guesses they can also be regal, royal, dark and strong. A manifestation of amber, the fuel that powers not just the Instars, but most of the world now.

Typically gold, the amber that fueled humanity's starward journey to colonize the rest of the Solar System can change in the presence of some people. Neither the military scientists nor the amateur investigators can answer why that happens.

Just as they cannot answer exactly why that amber turns human beings into Imago. There are theories, of course, thoughts that put the change into a similar realm as an overdose, the idea that the body can only take so much of a foreign substance before it reacts. In this case an alien substance. Some theorize it's psychological, that it has to do with a person's mental state when coming into contact with the amber. Metaphysical. Alien. The theories are endless.

Eric knows *how* the change happens, faces the danger of it himself as an Instar pilot, someone constantly in close proximity to the amber. Drilled into him a thousand times not just over his training, but his existence as a person in this world. The posters that line the streets, the educational videos they watch in school. Lines from his training that Eric memorized and could recite in his sleep. Improper exposure to other kinds of fuel, gasoline, electricity, coal, nuclear materials, and you were liable to kill only yourself. Improper exposure to the amber and you were liable to kill others as well, in ways too horrible to imagine. A blessing and a curse; a power source that brought humanity both its greatest tools and its greatest temptations.

Generations ago, thick veins of amber were discovered beneath the earth, an energy source far more effective and green than fossil fuels could ever hope to be. Those deposits were marked by enormous laureli trees the size of redwoods, their trunks twisted as if they spun in place as they grew. The energy produced by these golden veins power many of the Solar System's more prosperous cities now. They fuel the rockets that take colonizers to Mars, that shield the Jovian cities from the planet's intense storms, that protect the miners on Pluto from its frigid chill. And these veins of amber power the Instar exoskeletons.

But like anything rare, anything powerful, only a select few have access to it.

As lavender light pulses in the mindscape around him, the machine around his physical body must be beginning to power up. He's inside the egg-like cockpit of his Instar, surrounded by gel that smothers him like amniotic fluid, his physical movements restricted so that his nerves can be redirected to power the Instar instead, just like the human body does to itself to prevent sleepwalking.

Images flicker in the darkness, illuminated by the purple glow of the slow-motion lightning. Fragments like dreams compiled from his subconscious, bursting to life as the void constructs itself: a recruitment poster looking down at him; Eric signing his name again and again on a stack of official military documents; his first sight of his new sleeping quarters. Each one a step closer to his dream of becoming an Instar pilot.

"You ready to do this?"

Eric turns—is that it? Is there such an action as a turn in this world?—in the direction of the voice, and sees Loretta. His trainer. A fellow pilot. She's a tall, muscular woman, skin just a couple shades lighter than Eric's own, hair shaved tighter than his, all the way down to stubble. She's naked, but smoke swirls around her chest and groin, as if Eric's mind has taken it upon itself to edit out her nudity.

Eric takes a deep breath. "Let's go."

"Flip the switch!" Loretta calls out.

Eric doesn't even have enough time for another thought before—

—ALL THE SENSORY information of the corporeal world slams back into him.

Part of him wishes he could have stayed in the void.

"Fisher?" a voice comes in right next to his own ear, transmitted by the gel inside the pilot's cockpit. They'd practiced communicating like this before, but it still catches him a little off guard. When he opens his eyes, he's not entirely Eric. His body extends beyond his nervous system and into the bio-mechanical limbs of Solanum, the two-story-tall Instar he's piloting. Not entirely machine. Not entirely object.

"Fisher, you in there?"

"Yeah," he says. "I'm here."

And he stands.

The bio-metallic knees lifting him up are not his own, the back supporting him not his, but nevertheless he stands. Solanum is a tall, sleek machine, with a tapered silhouette, an upside-down triangle for a torso that connects to wide hips and long, lithe legs. It is strange to actually *feel* these things, to exist in another body. The Instar simulators offered sensations similar to this, but this feels completely and totally real, like his senses are no longer smothered or dulled, his receptors all cranked up to one hundred percent.

He lifts her hands, raises Solanum's hand to her face. Instead of the strong line of his own jaw, the stubble on his cheek, he finds a sleek, soft curve. It's smooth, hairless, the angle softer and rounder than his own. Previous generations' exosuits were made of cold, hard metal, but Solanum's body, like the other new constructs, are made from a bio-organic material developed for Instars. It has the same give, the same feel, as human skin—part of the engineers' attempt to lessen the supposed psychic damage from being in a foreign body. Solanum can't get goosebumps, but Eric expects he has them.

He notices a stranger sensation. A forty foot tall exosuit designed for military combat has no need for a penis.

For genitalia of any kind. It feels odd, that empty space. Her pelvis is smooth, like that of an action figure. Eric wants to explore what that sensation makes him feel but he's in the middle of a military exercise. People are watching him.

Solanum was designed not as a brawler, but for movement. As such, she possesses four sets of jet thrusters; on her back, her palms, the soles of her feet, and the backs of her calves. The jets don't allow her to fly—that would take much more thrust to get something as heavy as an Instar up into the air—but they keep her balanced, give her enough maneuverability to turn her into a brilliant lavender blur of motion during a fight. Eric spent hours pouring over the compiled recordings of Nasrin Addai, Solanum's previous pilot, moving the Instar across various battlefields in a beautiful purple ballet. He committed those movements to memory, determined to emulate them.

"Earth to Fisher."

Eric turns Solanum's head. Loretta looks back at him across the familiar wide open rock quarry from behind the eyes of her own Instar, Brassica. Brassica is taller than Solanum, sturdier. Wide hips and broad shoulders built to hold the stash of melee weapons on her back: axes and swords. Thick arms that remind him of Loretta's human ones. A brilliant green-and-yellow pattern. In Eric's childhood, at the beginning of the war, all the Instars were dark-colored, gunmetal grays and bush greens like other military vehicles. When their construction methods changed, the engineers decided to use the same bright colors that served as a warning in nature, so they would serve as a warning to the Imagos, unnerve them. If it were even possible to unnerve such creatures.

Brassica's face certainly unnerves Eric. Her eyes are an unsettling maroon, a reflection of Loretta's cosmic color.

"You good?" Loretta asks, and Eric nearly stumbles as that reassuring voice comes out of Brassica's bizarre, mouthless face.

"Yeah. I'm good."

Brassica takes up a fighting stance, her fists raised up.

"Then let's go. Remember, trust your gut when you're fighting. This," she says, gesturing to Solanum, "is your body too. Trust it."

This is what they're here for, after all. No more training in ten- or twenty-times Earth's gravity. This was time for the real thing. One final test, and the reality of that comes back to Eric, that he is very nearly an official Instar pilot. Just one last test.

Moving Solanum's body is immediately second nature to Eric. All he has to do is think about moving her hand and her hand moves. He doesn't have to send electrical signals down his nerve endings, it just happens. The jets on Solanum's soles activate, lifting her just off the ground. The jets on her back and the back of her calves fire next, blasting Eric forward towards Brassica. The jets on her palms fire at a lower intensity. He uses them to steer, shooting forward just above the ground. Coming in low. Eric has been in enough fights in his own body, he knows what to do when you have an enemy bigger than yourself.

Loretta notes his angle, and braces with Brassica, bringing her low to the ground to avoid Solanum's sweep. She catches Solanum in her arms and wraps her up in a bear hug. Solanum's sensory inputs relay every inch of Brassica's power to Eric as she lifts Solanum up and crushes her. Solanum's left arm is caught at a particularly odd angle, and Eric can feel the pressure crushing down on it, wondering how they made the pain receptors so real.

"Seen that one before," Loretta laughs, squeezing harder.

"Seen this one before?" He fires the thrusters on Solanum's back, enough to tip the top-heavy Brassica. Loretta's Instar doesn't fall over, not entirely, but it's enough to make her wobble and take a step backwards, to loosen her grip as she tries for balance. He fires the thruster on the back of Solanum's right calf. Her knee shoots up. Catches Brassica under the chin and knocks her back.

That's enough to break free.

Eric lands Solanum nimbly. Presses his advantage as Brassica staggers. He uses Solanum's speed, her size, to his advantage. Gets inside Brassica's reach. Rolling, firing her jets at every opportunity to maximize speed or quickly course-correct. All around the sparring Instars, the ground shakes. Boulders fall from the walls of the quarry, crashing to the dirt around them. They fight with everything they have. Eric can tell, finally, after all their matches together, Loretta isn't taking it easy on him. Isn't pulling Brassica's punches, isn't holding back. And Eric is actually coming out on top.

He's going to win.

He sees an opening. Drops Solanum to the ground. Slides between Brassica's legs. Pulls her feet out from under her. She falls, and he directs Solanum to snatch a sword from Brassica's back. Fires her jets. Spins. Comes to a stop with the sword drawn, tip pointed right at Brassica's throat.

Solanum stops, sword drawn, angled over Brassica's heaving chest. He imagines his own is puffed forward, doing the same. He can smell Solanum's bio-organic sweat, the dirt and grime from the quarry, the thruster-scorched earth. Solanum's left arm is bleeding, leaking lavender, but the adrenaline flowing through Eric has blocked the pain.

Below him, Loretta says, "Nice job." And then, "I think you're ready."

ERIC WISHES HE could stay for just a bit longer, has to focus on not outwardly displaying his anxiety at having to leave Solanum. The gel surrounding him goes from deep red to a cooler yellow. It holds there for a moment, and then Eric's stomach drops out from under him as the egg-shaped cockpit falls and Eric is ejected out of Solanum along with the viscous, yellow gel. The gel sloshes everywhere, and the cold air of the hangar dances its fingertips across his skin. He's back on the *Daedalus*, one of the many military airships used to train Instar pilots. Eric's home for the past several months.

A whole team of people swarm the scene like a colony of ants, each one knowing their purpose. The BSS pit crew, standing by until Eric and Loretta come spilling out of their Instars. One of the crew members lifts him up and pulls off the oxygen mask fitted around his face, another hands him a towel, and a third begins checking his vitals.

At first, he can't quite tell who it is that's attending to him, because his senses are still split, fifty-fifty, between Eric and Solanum. Two input sources for everything.

"Hey, pal." Both Eric's and Solanum's eyes turn towards crewmember Anthony Wedge, Solanum's eyes observing from above, watching Eric watch Wedge.

The sprinkling of white in Wedge's hair offsets his young features and makes him appear older than he is. He's known Eric since he first began getting in and out of simulators. Wedge holds a tablet in his hands, thick and brick-like, like most BSS tech, designed for durability.

"Ready to de-tether?"

"If I have to," Eric says. He looks down at his hand, flexing his fingers, just as Solanum looks down at hers.

"Hold there, bud." Wedge circles around Eric to his back. Eric watches through Solanum's eyes. Attached to the entire length of his spine, from waist to the base of his skull, is a long, metallic device. The device resembles a segmented carapace, which is why long ago pilots dubbed it *the centipede*, and the name stuck. Eric knows the carapace has an official designation, the Pilot to Instar Telemetry unit, the PiT, but only the techs actually call it that.

The centipede is thinner at the base, widening towards the top. Protruding from every segment, tiny, acupuncture-sized needles penetrate Eric's skin, lancing directly into his nervous system. From the device's back side, long, rope-thick wires protrude up and away, into Solanum's cockpit, disappearing up into her internal wiring like a series of robotic umbilical cords.

While connected, the centipede links pilot and Instar, Eric and Solanum. Anything he does, she will do. It's the most important part of an Instar. Eric has seen training videos of the exosuits functioning, albeit temporarily, without limbs or even a head, so long as the pilot can withstand the mental strain of the pain. But without the centipede, there's nothing linking an Instar to its pilot, and it becomes a useless, two-story skeleton. For that reason its connective tissue is hidden deep within the guts of the Instars, in the center mass, more protected even than a human spine. Lose the centipede, lose the battle.

In preparation for Eric disembarking, Wedge has turned what is normally a two-way street between pilot and Instar into a single lane. Wedge counts him down.

"Three…two…one…offline."

A light inside Eric goes out.

Everything Eric felt through the lens of Solanum snaps out of existence. Without that input, he begins to notice the wet grating beneath his human feet. The coldness of the room, amplified by the gel covering him, spreads goosebumps across his skin. The cacophony of the hangar bouncing off his eardrums. The humming of the electricity.

The heavy weight of his own muscles settles over him. His bones ache. He feels the wet hair on his head, the scratchy stubble on his face, the ringlets of hair on his chest. He's acutely aware of the sensation of his member dangling between his legs, shrunken in the cold. The awareness is irritating and insistent, a sensory overload.

He is, once again, entirely Eric.

Being suddenly back in his own body disorients him and he staggers, but Wedge braces him to keep Eric from falling. Eric wants to thank him, not just for doing his job, but for being a decent human. But Wedge's gloves, his sleeves, feel rough and grating against Eric's skin, and it distracts him enough that he untangles himself as soon as he can get his feet properly under him.

"Thanks," Eric says, because it's all he can say. Not just because he can't articulate the rest, but because a part of him tells him he shouldn't, that feelings like that are best kept inside.

"No problemo. Ready for removal?"

Eric nods.

Wedge shuffles behind him and counts down again. When he gets to one, he removes the centipede. It's not a painful sensation, exactly, but it is certainly a *lot*, dozens of needles sliding out of him, leaving him cold, feeling empty for some reason. Like something should be there that isn't.

You've wanted this your whole life, Eric tells himself. *Ever since you saw what you could be.*

Across the hangar, Brassica crouches in the standard eject position: on its knees, leaning forward, palms on the ground. Loretta is already halfway out, the oval, cocoon-like cockpit sprouting out of the Instar where a human's navel would be. Bullet- and shatter-proof glass on the cockpit slides up, and the amniotic gel Loretta had been floating in splashes out onto the hangar floor, drips through the grates below.

Biggs, another crew member, a hefty guy with a pushbroom mustache, attempts to help Loretta out of her Instar, but she doesn't need it. She lands on her feet gracefully. There's a loud ringing as her muscled mass comes crashing down to the metal grate. As in the void, Eric catches himself looking at her. Not at her nudity, but at the swelling of her hips. At her upper arms. The way her waist tapers inward. Her six-pack. The classical androgyny of her form.

Loretta stands tall, her centipede still connecting her to Brassica. She spots Eric and gives him a thumbs up. He shoots her one right back.

Body dysmorphia is a side effect of Instar piloting, Eric knows. It's one of the first things pilots are taught during training, before they even leave the classroom. After entering an Instar, navigating the world from within a completely different body, you will emerge with a distorted self-image. There are no amount of simulator exercises that can truly prepare you. Still, Eric and the other cadets were taught how to manage the feelings that come up, were told they are not real, just side effects of literally being someone else. Synchronicity with an Instar is a good thing, signals proficiency as a pilot. But every soldier needs downtime. Eric tries to shake those dysphoric feelings loose, remind himself of where he is and who he is inside, and then wonders why he thinks of it like that. Inside.

Biggs hands Loretta a towel but she uses it to wipe the fluid from her face, spitting some onto the floor. Eric is fascinated by how she refuses to hide her body, surprised he doesn't have to hide himself, turn away, drape something over his lower half.

Stop it, he tells himself, *that's just the side effects of piloting talking.*

Loretta strides confidently across the hangar, still toweling off with muscular arms.

"Excellent work, pilot."

Pilot. Eric does the best he can to remain upright, wobbling on fawn legs. Before this moment he has always been *cadet*.

Loretta holds out a hand.

"Your graduation will make it official, of course," she says. "But I think it's okay to say welcome to the ranks, Pilot Fisher."

Eric wipes his hand off on his towel. Loretta's grip is as firm as Eric expects. A grip that pulls him entirely back into his body when all he can think about is the next time he'll get to pilot Solanum.

ERIC, JUST ERIC, sits in one of those paper-lined doctor's benches with a towel over his shoulders. Waiting in a small, chilly exam room for his post-ejection physical. There's a few last Ts to cross before Eric can *officially* call himself Pilot Fisher, and one of them is a final series of physical and mental examinations. The first time he ever went through it, the doctor told him, *We just want to make you're still you.* Eric could guess what that meant, what it implied about the mental strain of the link to the simulator and the Instar. But he's not sure *him* is right. It seems like the nerves on his body aren't ever in proper working order when he's Eric. His senses are buried under a layer of cotton. But as Solanum he feels it all, as he was meant to.

Eric supposes a checkup for such a thing shouldn't be out of the question. People get addicted to drugs, food, television, video games, cell phones, sex, social media. He's heard of the color clubs people go to recreationally

explore one another's mindscapes, to traipse through
their own versions of the void he experienced before
inhabiting Solanum. Eric is nervous. Addiction would be
unfitting of a pilot, of the man he's trained most of his life
to be. Sitting there in the exam room, anxiety has Eric
in its grip. He bounces his leg, eyes darting around the
empty room, trying to take in the details about the room
instead of lingering on his own body: posters about pain
levels and numbers to call for confidential therapy groups
hovering above him, the lifeless CRT computer monitor
on the desk on the other side. He tries not to think about
how there's no wound on his forearm when Brassica bear-
hugged him. No mark on his skin to suggest anything ever
happened at all.

He straightens up his posture when the door opens
and a doctor comes in, a tall blonde woman he hasn't met
before. Being in the military, and especially in a division
controlled by the secretive Bureau of Special Services, is a
constant cycle of new faces. Eric knows he's too attached
to Loretta, but he barely knows his classmates. They will
all deploy to different assignments, when the time comes.

The doctor tests Eric's reflexes, asks him the same questions
about his body and his mind all the other doctors have. He
answers them quickly and concisely, without meeting her
eye, cognizant of the fear someone like her implicitly bears
from someone like him, despite clearly having more societal
power. She tells him to close his eyes, asks him to describe
his own physical form. He imagines himself spread out like
the Vitruvian Man, a Black butterfly under display, and he
wonders if, in this moment of being unobserved, her eyes slide
over him in the same hungry way past doctors' eyes have. She
records all his answers by pecking loud, plastic keys on the
keyboard before the CRT monitor.

Most of the visit is straightforward. She taps Eric on the
knees with one of those little, plastic hammers. Tiny pokes
and prods everywhere. She wraps a sleeve around his arm

and tests his blood pressure. She takes two vials of his blood, makes sure he's up to date with all his vaccinations. But when she gently prods the tiny acupuncture-esque holes the centipede contraption leaves behind in his spine, it sends odd, pleasurable sensations all across Eric's back. He tries to hide that reaction from her, but she flinches at the sight of his pleasure and jots something down.

Finally the doctor touches a device like a chunky television remote to the side of his neck. After the bite of the needle, she reads the result displayed on the device's face with a noncommittal huff, which tells Eric the amber levels in his body are nominal. He is not in danger of any transformation. No overdose, no simple mathematical threshold for him to stay away from. He thinks about the other theories of Imago transformation, the quantum physics explanations of this alien material that are beyond him, the idea that the amber might be some form of life we do not yet understand. The only theory he truly understands is the psychological one, the thought of unrest, of unresolved issues. Eric doesn't have to worry about that, even if it's true. He's right where he should be.

When the doctor is finished with the physical, they move on to the psych eval. "What's your name?"

"Eric Fisher."

"What is your rank?"

"Cadet." One step away from what he's wanted to be for his entire life. Since he was a child, Eric has always been hungry for the respect they garnered, the adoration people gave them.

"Of?"

"The Instar Solanum." He remembers thinking things could be different for him if he enlisted. Things could be *better.*

"Where are we now?" The doctor's voice has a strange inflection he's not prepared for, like she's getting to know him on a blind date.

"Aboard the airship *Daedalus*."

The doctor nods. "How long since you enlisted?"

"When I was nineteen." Enlisting meant that his higher education was paid for, along with his parents' house and most of their debts. "Becoming a pilot was always the goal."

Now come the pictures.

The doctor loudly clacks some keys on her keyboard and the CRT image changes with an audible click. She asks Eric to say, in one word, the first thing that comes to his mind, measuring his vitals as he responds. With each response the doctor jots down a note by loudly clacking keys. He barely registers the first few images until she shares a vintage image of Black soldiers posing for a portrait. Probably from World War I or II, hundreds of years ago. Before the cosmic color, before the colonization of the Solar System, before the Instars, and before even their huge, clunky exosuit precursors. Eric wonders if those men felt the same as him, if they felt they could elevate themselves, prove themselves, by joining. He wonders if things were different for them after they came home. They had to have been.

"Brave."

Next: a squadron of police officers facing something offscreen. The blue uniforms hit Eric with a small spike of anxiety, but he concentrates on what he's supposed to feel, what he's been trained to feel.

"Danger."

A flock of ships blasting off from the Earth, moving out to colonize the Solar System, a miracle once thought impossible, made true by the color.

"Destiny."

A cocoon of something like a moth.

"Transformation."

A picture of Solanum.

Eric can almost feel his blood pressure spike. For the first time, he hitches on a word. "Safety."

The doctor makes a note. Shows him the final image. A portrait, not a picture, of a nearly nude woman lounging on a chaise, a sheet covering her breasts, her crotch. A lump forms in Eric's throat. He knows now the doctor notices his vital signs changing, but neither of them acknowledges it.

"Beautiful."

The doctor lifts her head. Studies him. Lowers her head. Writes a note.

"Okay," she says. She slaps on a smile as if suddenly remembering to, as if thinking *ah, yes, this is how humans interact.* Like the other doctors, she's completely unreadable. For a moment, Eric has no idea if he passes or not. But whatever it is she writes, when she looks up from her notes, she smiles, and says, "Congratulations, Pilot Fisher," and Eric can't help but think that he has somehow cheated on this exam without even knowing it.

ERIC SECURES HIS cufflinks, makes one final adjustment on his tie, and meets his reflection's gaze in his small bunkroom's mirror, quickly wiping away the grimace he finds there. The unit's barber shaved him and gave him a haircut for the occasion, according to the ceremony's dress code. Eric leans closer into the mirror, bending over the small sink jammed into the corner of his bunkroom between his nightstand and his door, inspecting each tiny follicle in his cheeks and neck. A familiar ritual. They sure got just about everything, a closer shave with an open blade than he has ever been able to get. For once, Eric doesn't find himself standing in front of the mirror for another hour, slowly tweezing every remaining hair out of its follicle.

The haircut, though, is a different story.

It's a soft fade, one that objectively frames his face handsomely, yet still doesn't feel quite like *him*. He's bothered that he doesn't like it. Eric turns around and around in the mirror, like he's done since childhood with every haircut, each new style, each attempt to comfort in his reflection. But yet again he finds no good angle.

At least the Bureau of Special Services's ceremonial armor looks good from every angle. The white breastplate with segmented, brown shoulder-straps. White gloves. A blue undershirt. Navy pants. White boots. It has a retrofuturist aesthetic, deliberately meant to evoke the space-suits of humanity's first forays out into the Solar System. Warmth swells in Eric's chest, despite not having even been alive at such a time. Nostalgia is a truly powerful too. It works even if you weren't there for it.

It's always worked for Eric. Ever since he was young, when he first saw one of the Imago on television, when one had appeared in the San Francisco Bay. Days later, they said it was one of the workers at a nearby amber processing facility who'd transformed, who'd hidden his affliction from his coworkers. It was the first time Eric's parents ever let him watch the news during an incident, and he thought he was about to see the Golden Gate Bridge for the last time.

But the creature was tiny. Well, comparatively. Nowhere near as big as he thought Imago were going to be. Not living, reptilian skyscrapers, not capable of destroying the Bridge. Not unless there were a thousand of them. From all the stories young Eric heard about the Imago, he'd expected monstrosities knocking over buildings. After all, people called them giants, monarchs, titans. He expected a force of nature, something that could wipe him off the planet without a second thought, something too big to even observe a human. But in reality, they were only a few stories tall.

At first, he was confused, but when he thought about it, it only made them scarier.

Eric, like any rational person, fears natural disasters, hurricanes, earthquakes, tornadoes. But only in the most abstract sense. If he were to die by a natural disaster, it would be impersonal. It would be over in the blink of an eye. There would be little he could actually do about it.

Disasters of that scale didn't make him afraid the same way he feared the dog that once chased him down an alley and over a fence when he was a boy. He still remembers the chain link biting into his hands, the hair raised on the back of his neck. Like those teeth were right behind him. He remembers the growls and barks of the dog as he climbed higher, the feeling of falling as he finally flipped over the top and to the other side. Nothing but a chain link fence separating them, the big animal barking and growling, pacing back and forth. Eric remembers knowing, intimately, what this animal would do to him if it caught him. All that for trying to take a shortcut home from school through the wrong street.

That day on the Bridge, BSS deployed one of the earlier-generation Instars—Napa—from the back of a WEAPON platform. Napa was a bright, green model. Short and stout. Equipped with heavy armor and dual shields in an approach that was called *aggressive defense*: let the enemy tire itself out against the shields, then go in for the kill. There used to be a boxer who did that, Eric remembers, hundreds of years ago.

Napa and the Imago—a reptilian thing that looked like a Basilisk lizard that stood on two legs, big, bulbous, chameleonic eyes—smashed their way through the San Francisco Bay, Napa struggling to take the Imago to land, where the pilot would have an advantage. Eric was sure he was about to watch someone die. The Imago tore into Napa's armor, breaking its shields, rending into its hull. Spurts of fizzing, evaporating turquoise flew everywhere, the fuel that powered the Instar. But at the last minute, Napa rallied and the pilot gained the upper hand.

Napa bashed the Imago with the remnants of its shields, pushing it towards shore. They narrowly avoided Alcatraz Island, the fight culminating on the beach, where Napa decapitated it with the jagged end of its shield.

Eric had to look away at the end. Just before the final blow. Remembering this monster was once a man. When it was over, in the aftermath, the pilot deployed, right there onto the beach, and Eric's heart leaped into his throat.

The pilot was Black.

Such a thing had never even occurred to Eric.

Like any other boy, Eric had been watching movies and television shows all his life. Every single time, whenever he saw a dark face on screen, he could always point out that they would either be the villain, or be there for a couple funny lines and then meet some gruesome end. Usually as motivation for the hero. The "real" characters. Even in the things he liked. And in those things he watched as a child, those stories that took place in fantasy worlds, he always had to struggle, to stretch his mind, and claim a character for himself where no other Black people were present. White people, sure. Aliens, of course. Creatures from other stars. Other dimensions. Dragons. Genies. Ghosts. Zombies. But no dark-skinned faces.

The pilot, who Eric later learned was named Darius Draven, strode out onto the beach of the San Francisco Bay, golden amber swirling around him like particulate matter, motes of dust in the air around him, unaffected by the cosmic color seeping into his pores. Maybe he simply hadn't been exposed to enough of the color to change him. Maybe it was psychological, and Draven was simply in control of himself in that moment. For whatever reason, the element's alien makeup simply didn't take hold, didn't change him, merely let Draven exist with an aura about him, like a newborn god.

From the safety of his living room, Eric watched medical personnel swarm Draven, but he batted them away.

Instead he waved towards the news drones, slowly
turning between every single one, the aura of his
color surrounding him like harmless flames. It was
that moment, seeing someone like him not just on the
battlefield, not just on the front line, but being a *hero*, that
truly made up Eric's mind. Despite his fear of fighting.
Despite his fear of the Imago. Despite the fact that he
knew, even at that age, how hard it was going to be. He
was going to be a pilot, and he wouldn't just bury all the
bad things he felt—he'd conquer them.

The blue uniform made it real. He was finally a pilot.

Maybe, as a pilot, things would be different.

Maybe this was the missing piece he needed.

THERE ARE OTHER cadets at the graduation ceremony, all
dressed in the same uniform as Eric, all standing stage
right, looking out at the massive auditorium. He supposes
they are pilots now. Or at least they will be in a matter
of minutes. He recognizes all of them, though he's spent
little time with them for the last few months, sequestered
as he was with Loretta. Like him, the other cadets had
all been assigned a full-fledged pilot as a mentor. Eric
wasn't especially friendly with any of them, but he'd
gotten to know a few. Sean Sabat, whose temper had to
be beaten into submission by his supervising pilot. There's
Christopher Schemmel, a quiet young man constantly
acing his scores.

But there's also Cassandra Vort, the undisputed hotshot
of the graduating class. Cassandra was already doing
BSS recruitment commercials, and her scores in an Instar
were unmatched by even the last few graduating classes.
Cassandra is a strong, blond woman with the sides of her
head shaved, her remaining hair gelled back.

She's got high cheekbones and stunning, sharp eyes that make Eric understand why she is the face of the recruitment posters. Eric and Cassandra had been friendly in classes together before their mentorships started, and had only had enough conversations for Eric to be intimidated by her singular focus on perfecting absolutely everything she did.

Eric turns away from her.

Loretta is in the audience sitting among other mentors and retired pilots, cadets' parents, various high-ranking BSS members, and family members. Eric knows he's not the first pilot Loretta has watched graduate, but he does like to think there's something different about him, something that sets him apart from the rest of the pack, even if he isn't the *best*, like Cassandra. Maybe everyone up on that stage is thinking that. That they're different, special in some unique way. They have to be, since the graduating classes for pilots are getting smaller and smaller every year. They have to stand out because there's not so many of them anymore. Public sentiment towards piloting has always been positive, but with so few left, it's not just looks of wonder staring back at him from those in the crowd.

The Instar pilots were the stars of the Bureau of Special Services. The BSS's applications of the cosmic color into exosuit technologies (initially designed to help people survive on the frontiers of galactic expansion) had always been at the cutting edge of scientific research and engineering, even more so now that the Instars are grown and molded meticulously from biomechanical flesh. It was a no-brainer to apply those technologies to stopping the emergence of the Imago. Fight fire with fire. Having a human-shaped weapon shake rubble off itself in the aftermath made the whole thing seem different. The Instars sweated when they exerted themselves. They bled their colors when they were injured. They brought the war that much closer to home, made everyone much more invested.

The older generation's purely mechanical suits couldn't do that.

At the height of their fame, BSS cadet classes had dozens of pilots on the stage every year. More than could possibly pilot all the Instars being manufactured. So some of them became explorers, pioneers, interplanetary police, leading colonization efforts on Titan or policing Mars. And those who became pilots, who became celebrities at the beginning of the war, they started doing what every soldier throughout history has done or will do at one point or another:

They died.

Many of them in the field. Sure, some graduated to higher ranks, leaving the field shortly before fading from the public eye, but Eric's graduating class is nine pilots. Including this class, there are forty-two active pilots for forty-two active Instars, with another dozen outdated units going through the decommissioning process.

The dean of the academy calls out a smattering of names throughout the auditorium before he reaches the Es and Eric straightens even further. When the head calls "Eric Fisher" into the microphone, Eric steps forward, doing exactly what he was told to do, exactly what he rehearsed with the other pilots and a thousand more times in his quarters. It's all mechanical. Memorized. Easy. He keeps his limbs straight, his body hardened. He walks across the stage. He's handed a rolled-up piece of paper he knows is little more than a prop diploma. Eric walks his practiced circle around the stage back to his seat, peering out into the audience for his family. For Loretta. He sees them, mother, father, teacher. Waving. Smiling. He does the same back. Sits down. Watches as the rest of the graduating class does the same circuit as him. Cassie. Sean. Christopher. The faces he recognizes but can't name. It's all so choreographed. Rehearsed. It's over so quickly. It's hard to think that this is what he was waiting for.

Eric fidgets in his seat.

WHAT HAPPENS NEXT isn't an official part of the ceremony, but Loretta told him it would happen, and there's no way Eric is missing it. As everything begins to wind down, he, along with the other graduates, heads down into the hangar, to where the Instars are housed. They take a freight elevator, the lot of them riding down with giddy anticipation, trying to remain composed as the huge double doors open up to reveal an even larger room, massive, football fields wide and four stories tall. The roof is retracted at the moment, showing them the sun, the clear blue sky. Eric knows the floor can ascend, lifting the Instars up to the flight deck just as with fighter planes. But in the meantime the open roof only lets in a soft breeze and the sunlight, filtering in and lighting the two parallel rows of Instars. The two-story machines all wait as if to greet them. Ladders—or in some cases entire scaffolding rigs for some of the bigger units—have been propped up. And atop each ladder stands a member of that unit's crew, working at some small detail on the units' surfaces.

Eric is aware of the other Instars, of the bright, poisonous yellow of Christopher Schemmel's Carinata, a smaller, dexterous Instar in the same vein as Solanum that wielded dual blades, of the copper sheen of Raphanus, a midrange support Instar that bore a large three-burst rifle. Eric doesn't know if he'll ever get used to the faces of the Instars. They're both too human and not human enough. Smack dab in the center of the uncanny valley. But even as some part of him wants to linger, he finds himself keeping as much distance as he can from all the other graduates, who give Eric a skin-crawling feeling he can't articulate. Like even though he's one of them now, he still isn't. Instead, he tries to focus all his energy on Solanum. She's different from this angle, standing below her, lit by the sun. She's on display. He's used to seeing Solanum from within, or from the range of a screen. Meeting her on the hangar floor is almost an out-of-body experience. Looking up at her now, he remembers something Loretta said to him the first time he ever saw one up close: *They figured out if they made them too big, what they stood for was incomprehensible. We need them to be real. Not forces of nature. Closer to human.*

Eric doesn't think such a thing could ever be close to human. He's never been a particularly religious person, but Instars always make him think of something angelic.

The first generations of mecha were vaguely human-shaped, traditionally-imagined exosuits made of thick, tank-like armor, no heads as humans imagine them, but merely a torso/cockpit in which the pilot sat, twitching joysticks to move the lumbering creations. Their robotic joints were visible, their bodies pockmarked with steps and handholds for their pilots to climb. Multifaceted eyes, like the lens of a drone, were affixed to small rotators all around the torso, giving a 360-degree view.

The Instars are both too human and not human enough.

The crew member standing atop a tall ladder, attending to something on Solanum's chest, is Wedge. He smiles when he sees Eric. "Hey, big shot. You're officially a pilot now, eh?"

Eric puffs out his chest without realizing he's doing it. A part of him thought that once he became a pilot, people would stop referring to him with supposedly-affectionate names like *big shot* or *kid*. But to some people, there's just something he will always be.

"Well, you're just in time." Wedge turns back, makes one more adjustment, his body still blocking Eric's view. "Check it out." He climbs down and out of the way so Eric can get a closer look. Running alongside Solanum's chest, right where the collarbone should be, there are now two words, like a tattoo: *SOLANUM - FISHER*.

A wave washes over Eric, stronger than he ever expected. Something bigger than pride, but he can't name it. He's been proud of himself for enlisting, for being accepted as a pilot, for completing his training, but this is something different. This is something deeper, stranger, stronger. A double-edged feeling he doesn't know the entirety of. He's here, he thinks, he's made it.

His name written on Solanum, their names together, it stirs something in him, something he can't find the words to articulate. The closest he can get is *rightness*. It feels right. Eric tries to dig down, dig deeper, but he can't find anything more articulate than that. It's like in the digging, in trying to find what it means, he's found himself boxed in.

The only thing he knows for sure is he wants to be piloting again. He doesn't just *want* to. He needs to.

A need he feels in his bones. Because it's the only thing that makes all the other feelings go away.

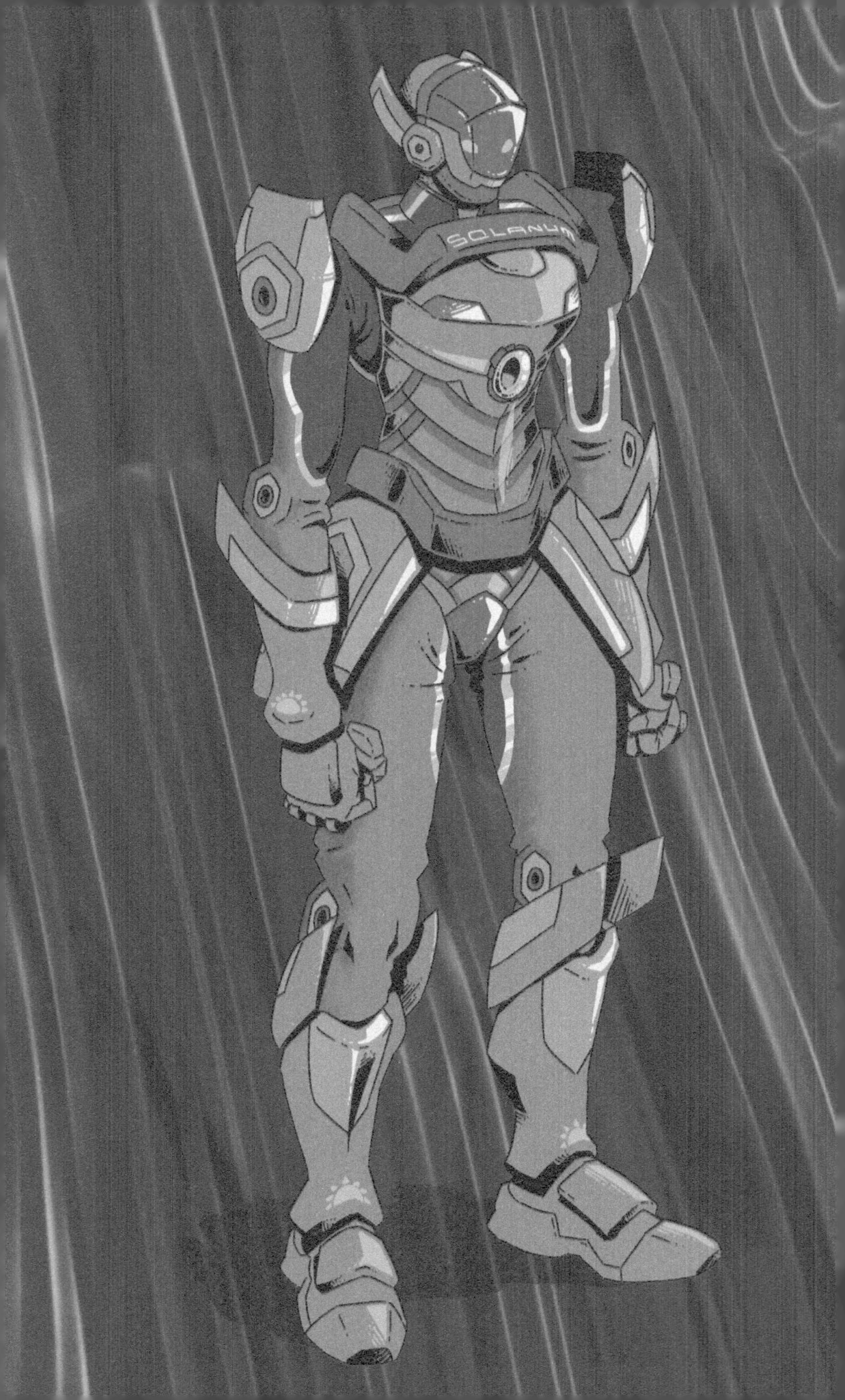
SOLANUM

CHRYSALIS

PART II

ERIC TWISTS AROUND in his landing craft seat, away from Loretta, from the other newly-minted pilots, back up at the *Daedalus*. He's constantly amazed at how something so enormous, a leviathan of steel and burning jet engines, manages to stay airborne. He's not often beneath the Bureau of Special Service's floating headquarters, and glares harder, longer, at the underslung gun turrets than he ever has before, the sight pitching an unexpected, anxious twinge in his stomach. He can't see the hundreds of high-powered, telescopic cameras dotted all over the *Daedalus'* underside, constantly pointed at the cities and highway and towns below its flight path, but he knows they're there. There is an uncanny absence of noise from such an enormous vessel, the way it hovers, completely silent. A miracle of engineering achieved by mastery of the cosmic color.

Are those guns the only things people on the ground see of the *Daedalus*? Do the sight of all those barrels make them feel safe, or do they experience the same strange anxiety Eric does?

"Airsick?"

Loretta furrows her brows and leans forward, strapped in across from him, giving him the same look as when he bailed out of the flight simulator on his second try, barely able to keep his lunch down. *Happens all the time, don't worry, it won't hurt your score. Never does.* "Eric?" she asks, and he knows she thinks it's serious because she uses his first name. "You alright?"

"Yeah." He's shocked at how easily the lie comes out. What's happening to him?

Some of his classmates glance his way, and Cassandra quietly posits how a pilot who gets queasy this easily is supposed to stand a chance when the real action starts.

Eric tries not to dread the events of Fleet Week they're flying down towards. The thought of hundreds of cameras pointed in his direction makes him feel very much the same way the guns on the underside of the *Daedalus*. Fixed. Stuck. In a danger he can't entirely comprehend. But then again he's never been much of a public person. Even giving presentations in front of his middle school classmates gave him the willies. He told himself that Darius Draven never felt his way. The other pilots with them—Cassandra, Christopher, Sean, everyone else— none of them show signs of any such nerves. Their eyes on him scratch like crawling, tiny pinpricks.

Cassandra's eyes linger. Eric expects her to pretend like she hasn't been caught. Instead, her chin tilts upwards. Only then does she move, and it's slowly, languidly, turning her gaze out over the city skyline coming up to meet them, pretending like she sees something interesting.

As the craft lowers, the din of the city rises towards them, patriotic marching band music filled with drums and brass, the shouts of an awaiting crowd. Eric turns his attention to the ground below. They're landing in the middle of a football field, the stands of the stadium coming up all around them.

The stadium is absolutely packed with people. Civilians crammed into the seats like it's a sold-out concert venue. Even from this distance, Eric can't deny the joy on their faces, the children trying to catch the eyes of their heroes, the adults looking out for their saviors. The onlookers have brought with them everything from Instar action figures and T-shirts to signs cheering the pilots on in their forthcoming battles.

While the civilians are restricted to the stands, the field itself is full of police, military personnel, and news crews. They wait patiently outside a ring of air traffic controllers who safely guide the landing craft to a soft stop.

When the craft lands, Eric waits for the other pilots to disembark before he steps out, reassured by the solid ground underneath his feet.

"Feels weird, huh?" Loretta asks. "Getting used to the ground again, I mean."

"Oh," Eric says, "Right." That's not all of it, and Loretta seems to know that.

"Your land legs will come back pretty quick," she says, giving him a small nudge. The awaiting crowd explodes as his descending classmates step into view, each one of them eating it up in a way Eric can't imagine himself doing. They smile and wave and cheer and pose for pictures. He only realizes he's still sitting down when Loretta puts a hand under his arm and pulls him up. "Come on, now," she says, calmly but sternly, "There are people waiting for us."

Eric is buffeted so hard with noise he almost recoils. He would have, if not for Loretta's hand on his shoulder. Her smile is amicable, camera-ready, but her single, hard squeeze says something else, and Eric straightens his posture and waves at the cheering faces. A mask slides up over his face, the same one he wore at the graduation and in the doctor's office. Something plastic and smothering that keeps all the heat in. When he moves, it's with the rigid, unarticulated marching of a simple action figure.

He follows the other pilots off the lander and onto the football field, and as Eric tracks the thousands of faces in the seats around them, he notices one group isn't chanting or cheering, aren't dressed in celebratory or summery clothing like the rest of the crowd. No, they're dressed for a funeral, all in black, their faces covered. Some of them wear veils, others simple surgical masks, but a couple of them wear much more intricate masks, handmade. Bugs and reptiles. Motionless mandibles and closed beaks.

They're masks of Imagos.

Eric knows these people. Not personally, but he's heard of them. Followers of the Book of the Metamorphosis, a text written hundreds of years ago in the wake of the first Imago emergences. Urban legends said the text was initially written on the chitinous shell of one of the first Imago. The book asked philosophical questions about the amber and the cosmic color, wondered if human transformation wasn't actually a gift from the universe as opposed to the curse most saw it is. They touted a combination theory about the Imagos and the color, intertwining the element's alien anatomy with humans' own psychology, believing people needed to reach a type of nirvana before being exposed, otherwise the amber would continue to morph their bodies. They weren't a dangerous group, supposedly, but the BSS made it absolutely clear that they were not sympathetic to pilots. It wasn't right to kill them. They should be trying to solve the problem by using the color itself, not simply resorting to violence. There were still people inside the Imago, they said. Eric supposed that could be a possibility, but the lives of the innocent people caught up in an Imago emergence seemed more important.

The masked people stare at Eric and the other pilots as they descend from the landing craft onto the field, then as they shake the proffered hands of high-ranking BSS officials, the city's mayor, and other diplomats. Event security stays close to the masked group, but they remain mostly still, only turning towards the pilots as they make their way through the crowd, continuing to shake hands, wave, pose for pictures, before heading into the tunnels that lead into the guts of the stadium.

But even in the dark, Eric can still feel those masked eyes watching him, and a vague sense of guilt settles over him.

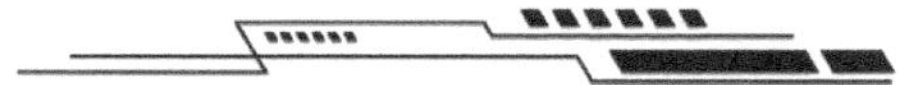

A WOMAN MEETS them in a conference room off from the tunnels beneath the stadium. The crowd outside continues to holler. Someone's on a megaphone making an announcement of some kind, but Eric can't tell what, the words warping into nothingness through distance. The drone of it all gives him a headache.

The woman waiting for them wears a standard BSS office uniform: heels, pencil skirt, a navy button-up with the BSS logo emblazoned on the shoulders, and tight epaulets. She has her hair pulled back into a bun, and carries a sturdy tablet in her hands, its body plastic-shielded, tough, like the rest of BSS technology. She stands at the head of a small, improvised BSS command center, staffed by soldiers in folding chairs typing away on thick-bodied computers settled on plastic tables. The room is filled with the familiar tone and tenor of military conversations, but to Eric it's all become white noise.

"Welcome back to the ground, pilots," the woman says, clicking a few buttons on the tablet's compact keyboard. "I have your itineraries here."

Another uniformed woman carries in a stack of bound reports. She glances at each pilot's name on their uniform before flipping through her collection of papers and handing them each a folder. When she's finished, she disappears back into the crowd as if she were never there.

"Everyone has something a little different," the first woman says, motioning to them to open their folders, "though sometimes there will be a little crossover. Mentors, don't worry, you'll be with your pilots for the majority of the time during Fleet Week, but everyone will have a handler who will tell them where to go at all times."

Eric scans his itinerary. There are a few items he expected, like the parade, a meet-and-greet, a photoshoot. It's strange to think his face might be used for a BSS recruitment poster the way Darius Draven's was. But then he stops cold.

MEETING W/ NASRIN ADDAI.

Nasrin Addai was Solanum's previous pilot, retired before Eric got a chance to meet her, long before he was assigned to Solanum. He didn't know much about her until he started watching videos of her trainings, her fights with the Imagos, to see how she handled the Instar. He'd needed to know how she moved, what Solanum was capable of, and who Eric would be walking in the footsteps of.

A meeting with Nasrin Addai. He wonders if she felt the same way about Solanum he does, that their connection is less like a pilot with a vehicle and more like one with another living being. After all those months of training, watching and rewatching all those archived videos, Eric has a sense of kinship with Addai, even though he doesn't know her. It isn't the same as what he feels with Darius Draven, but there's a connection through their respective tethers to Solanum. He has so many questions to ask, but even as they swirl around in his head, the possible answers frighten him.

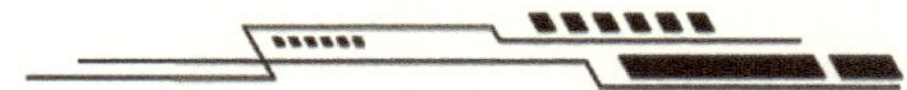

THE DAYS ON the ground blow by in a blur. Eric and the other pilots are whisked from event to event, with barely a moment to breathe between. He's coming down in the lander, at the stadium, then the next thing he knows they're part of a long motorcade, driving through the city. "Wave, don't just sit there," Loretta says, as they pass even larger crowds outside the stadium.

The sea of faces makes Eric queasy, confronted by their joy. But that's not right—it's not the kind of look someone gets when they come face-to-face with their favorite sports star. He doesn't react the way he always thought he would. Their expression is one of relief, and that realization makes him sink down into his seat a little more.

"CLOSER," THE PHOTOGRAPHER says. "Pretend like you like each other." The photographer stands at the edge of the bright stage, camera pointed at Eric and Cassandra, aperture clicking rapid-fire, pinning Eric amidst the backdrop and the fans and those big, white light reflectors.

"Come on," Cassandra says, sidling closer to him, "I won't bite." Eric's skin itches. Cassandra pulls him close. She takes his arm and wraps it across her waist. Fire lights across his skin.

"There we go," the photographer says, firing off a series of shots that sound like automatic gunfire. He shoots them from all angles: straight ahead, from the side, lying on the ground, telling them that last angle, especially, is what people want to see. "They want to be looking up at you," he says while Eric tries to adjust the natural double-chin that comes with such a pose. "As if you're coming down to save them."

The photographs are for recruitment ads, but Eric can't imagine the purpose of a shot where he's made to stand behind Cassandra, his right hand in his pocket, his left on her hip. She leans backward into him until her head rests on his shoulder. Even though Cassandra's arms are crossed in front of her, Eric feels hot, uncomfortable.

The photographer manipulates them into various poses, adjusts their uniforms, unbuttons their jackets for some more informal shots. They go through a dozen outfit changes, taking hundreds of photographs in each outfit, dozens of different poses each time. Sometimes they take a break and put Cassandra through hairstyle or makeup, curling or straightening her hair, or tucking it under a cap and throwing a wig on her. For every new set of pictures they put a different face on her. The photographer stands in front of Eric from time to time, considering his face, his hair, despite the wardrobe changes, saying, "Well, there's not really much we can do with this," at Eric's shaved scalp, and then adding, almost as an afterthought, "Not that we need to. I think it works."

They put Cassandra into a sleeveless, strapless green dress that ends just below the knee and the photographer wraps Eric's left hand around her waist, manipulates her and the stool she's half-standing on so it seems like Eric is carrying her in one arm.

"Hang on," the photographer says, running across the room to a box full of props. He returns with a ceremonial sword and says, "Hold this." He takes a step back and looks at his handiwork, then replaces it with a prop rifle. The nonexistent weight of it is empty and hollow, too easy to hold.

Eventually, the photographer steps back to survey the work with his crew.

"What is this?" Eric finally asks. The photographer doesn't hear him, busying himself with reviewing the last set of shots on his camera's screen. "Don't worry about it," Cassandra says, her tone low and concerned. "They just take everything they even think they need while they have us. Most of it doesn't even get used, just collects dust on a hard drive somewhere."

Gone is any of the sultry purr from before, or the snark from the lander. She turns away from Eric, as if to hide the sight of her in that green dress. She meets his eye over her shoulder, but Eric can't help noticing the strong muscles of her shoulders and back, the roundness of her backside. Eric can't figure out who she is beyond the image of a hotshot pilot, the idea of the person the military has created. But here before him is the *actual* person, albeit glammed up.

"What's your deal?" Eric asks. And then, aware of how sudden and strange that sounded, adds, "Why are you being so nice to me?"

"You think I'm nice?" Cassandra raises her eyebrows.

Is she actually flirting with him, or is that just her personality? "I really don't know what you are," Eric says.

Judging by her expression, the wry smile curling up the side of her mouth, she knows exactly what he means. Cassandra twirls her finger around her, indicating the whole photoshoot. "Some of this isn't even for the military. You think this dress," she says, popping her hip out, "is for a recruitment poster?" She shakes her head. "Nah, they'll probably digitize a cocktail or a bottle of perfume or who the hell knows what else into my hand."

"What?" Eric asks. "Can they do that?"

Cassandra laughs, and it's bright and genuine. "Oh, honey, didn't you read the fine print when you joined? That body of yours is theirs to do whatever they want with."

"What are you talking about?"

Cassandra sighs, exasperated. "This body," she says, gesturing to him, "is *theirs* now. They can do whatever they want with it. Slap it onto recruitment posters. Sell it to companies who want to sell sports drinks or medicine or clothes. Take your pick. You've seen the pictures of me modeling underwear, right?"

When Eric says he hasn't, Cassandra brings it up on a production assistant's personal phone. In the photos, Cassandra lounges across a couch, languid in a sheer set of lingerie, hooked to black stockings by a garter belt. Eric looks away, cheeks flushing, but he forces himself to take it all in.

"You think that's really me?" she asks.

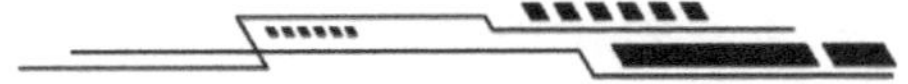

Eric strides stories above the crowd as Solanum. Ahead of him, a military convoy leads the way through the city, nameless lieutenants and generals ranked so far above him Eric doesn't need to know their names. Tanks are escorted through the streets by police cars, and Eric heads the procession of following Instars. The sidewalks and buildings and rooftops are choked with people. Lunatus and Brassica march directly behind him.

"Eyes front, Fisher," Loretta says, and Eric turns to watch where he's going.

The stares and the accolades are less strange inside Solanum. His thoughts keep drawing him back to Cassandra, to how close the photographer had pushed them. Moments ago, they both stood naked in front of one another, not in the hangar of the *Daedelus*, but on the tarmac of an airport as they prepared for the parade with their entire graduating class Instead of dissociating through the casual nudity like he usually did, he found himself staring at Cassandra.

She was right. That body in the lingerie ad was certainly not hers. The woman in that ad was stick thin, all ribs and jutting collarbone. Cassandra's actual body, on display as a technician attached her centipede, is firm, all hard muscle, defined abdominals and curving biceps. Eric averts his eyes as she boards Lunatus, but not before she notices him looking.

The parade passes in a haze, discomfort and distraction warring with the enjoyment that piloting brings him. He tries to find joy in the cheers, but too often they sound like screams.

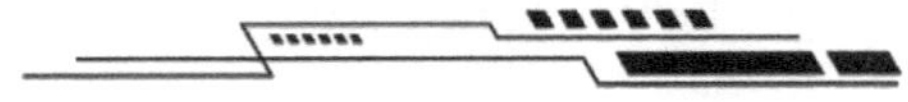

After the parade is over and he's disembarked, Eric stands under the steam of the shower, letting the warm water run the gel off his body. When he's finished, he wraps himself in a towel and stares at his reflection with a clinical detachment. Lines of muscle and a hairy chest where there should be a smooth chassis. Dark brown skin and a slim waist instead of a deep purple across thinner waist and broader shoulders. Is this the dysphoria they meant? Or is it Cassandra's fault, for showing him that lingerie-clad body that wasn't really hers. Will they do that to Eric too? He grows hard under his towel remembering the her-that-wasn't-her. "Hey," someone says, and he jumps. Cassandra peers out from around the corner, a towel wrapped around her. How long has she been standing there? How long has he? She wipes her mouth and then her forehead, catching the last running drips from the shower. "What do you got next?"

Eric has memorized his itinerary.

"Another photo op at a high school. With their ROTC program. You?"

"Christening a new airship," she says, clearly unenthused about it. "The escorts are downstairs."

"Cool," he says, even more unenthusiastic than Cassandra. He wonders how long she's going to stand there.

"I freak you out with all that body image stuff?" She gestures to the mirror.

"No," Eric lies.

"Sorry," she says, leaning against the wall. "If it's any consolation you'll barely see the kind of shit they make with you."

"Ignorance is bliss?"

"You'll be selling basketball shorts or energy drinks or gold chains or something. They won't spread you out on a couch like they did me." And then, looking him up and down, "Too bad."

He's both flattered by the attention and repulsed by it, the things they'll use his body for, the things she knows, whether she's aware of it or not. *Basketball shorts or energy drinks or gold chains.* "But that's not actually you on that couch."

"It's no big deal," Cassandra says. She gestures to Eric's arm. "You okay?"

He hadn't even noticed he was fidgeting with it. Eric continues to grace his fingertips over where his arm should have been injured, the place he felt that cracking pressure in his sparring session.

"Oh," he says, forcing himself to let go of it. "Yeah, I'm fine."

"I saw your tapes," Cassandra says. "It's weird, right? As if there should be a wound there?"

"Yeah." He swallows. "You ever feel like…you're not supposed to be here? Like…your body isn't your body?"

Cassandra breathes deeply, visibly softening. "I fell on a rock during mine," she says. "A boulder, really." She pushes her right knee forward, thigh creeping out from between the folds of her towel. She grabs the towel with her hand and pulls it back further, showing Eric a small, yellowing bruise on her thigh, but also the soft crease in her body where her leg meets her pelvis.

He swallows, trying to look only at the bruise.

"Then how did you…?"

"Slammed it into a table," she says. "On purpose."

Eric doesn't need to ask why.

She takes a step closer and reaches out, wrapping her hand around his forearm. He doesn't ask *what are you doing.* He doesn't stop her. He meets her eyes as she exerts a little pressure, her hands deceptively strong.

"It might be weird," she says, her voice lower, "but it helps." She squeezes tighter, holding his gaze. "Better?"

He nods.

"You wanna know how you fix that feeling?"

Does he *want* to fix it? Eric's not sure. "How?"

"By putting yourself back in this body."

Cassandra puts her lips on his before Eric can react. He's gasping, mouth open, giving her tongue an opening. It slides into him, playing with his own. Cassandra pulls herself closer, her breasts and stomach pressing against Eric's body through their towels. She's right—he's right here, completely present. Hard.

When she finally pulls her lips away, body still pressed against his, she asks, "Feel that?"

He does, he feels it all, but it's too much sensory input to parse out at once. He wants her, but it's like when she told him he'd signed away his body. Good and bad, too overloaded to fully process either.

"That's you," she says. "You want to feel me?"

"Yes," Eric breathes, even though he isn't sure. As Cassandra touches his chest, he glances over her shoulder into the bathroom mirror, needing to get a sense of himself, to ground himself, to remind him this is you and this is what's happening.

But when he looks in the mirror, he's not him.

He's Solanum.

She is the same height as Eric, standing there in the middle of the bathroom as Cassandra drops to her knees. Coming closer. Her hands on Solanum's hips, pulling the towel away entirely. But why? There's nothing down there for her. Just the empty, smooth curve of an Instar pelvis. But he can nevertheless feel Cassandra's mouth on him. Eric screws his eyes shut. Struggling to find something to do with his hands, he reaches forward, wrenches his fingers into Cassandra's hair. Harder than he expected to. Driven by anxiety. She makes a muffled gasp of approval. Eric gets harder, hotter, without his brain's permission. His dick is swelling, and something else takes over his limbs like he's switching to autopilot. He pulls Cassandra to her feet, drool penduluming off her lip. She knows what Eric wants, or what he's convinced himself he's supposed to want, and together they prop her up on the bathroom sink, her towel puddled on the floor. They grab one another, grasping and moaning, until Eric grabs her hips and Cassandra coaxes him inside her using their motion.

It's glorious and overwhelming and not enough and too much and he's finally alive even as he might just somehow also die. He wraps his arms around Cassandra as she does the same to him, each crushing into the other as if they can meld together into one person. She hooks her ankles together behind his back, matching his motion as he thrusts inside her. Eric loses himself in the morass of limbs, not sure where he ends and she begins. Cassandra peels a hand away from his back to rub herself. Eric tries to hold on, but it's only a matter of moments before he comes, thrusting harder inside her. A couple seconds later, as he's still shuddering, Cassandra climaxes, her muscles twitching and spasming, wrapping tight around him.

"It's okay," Cassandra says from somewhere. He's still inside her, and she still has her limbs around him, but he's only just starting to be able to differentiate between their bodies again. "It's okay," she says again, and Eric realizes she means him coming inside her. "I'm on birth control."

"Oh, I'm sorry I—"

"Jesus," she gasps, not listening. "I knew guys like you could fuck like that." She slowly peels herself away from him, and Eric steps back, struck by one final spasm of confusing pleasure as he leaves her body, eliciting a little gasp from them both.

"Guess we gotta take another shower," Cassandra says. Eric swallows.

"It's okay, catch your breath." She slides off the sink, knees wobbling. "Ooh, goddamn." She walks past him and turns the shower knob, stepping under a warm spray.

Eric joins her after a long moment.

"When's the last time you got any?" she asks with a laugh.

He hooked up with an old high school girlfriend during shore leave last year, and he tells her so. But there's a coldness there, in both that memory and this present, as Cassandra's words from earlier settle poorly in his gut. *Guys like you.*

"God, it's been years for me," she says, grabbing a washcloth and wiping between her legs. She doesn't even turn away from him. "Relax, Fisher," she says when she sees his expression. "I'm not asking you to go steady or anything. It's just a little sport fuck between friends."

AFTER WHAT HAPPENED in the shower, despite her comment, Eric can't stay away from Cassandra. Or maybe it's that he cannot escape her. The BSS escorts drive him to his ROTC meeting, during which he shakes hands with students and teachers alike. They ask him about what it's like to be a pilot, how hard the training was, if he's ever fought any Imago yet. They ask him what it's like to pilot a craft that doesn't use a joystick. They ask him about his fellow pilots. They ask him about the ace pilot, Cassandra.

He returns to the hotel at the end of the night and finds her at the bar. They don't talk about the bathroom—not directly anyway—but the edges of their conversation reflect in each other's eyes. Three drinks deep, she tells him to wait ten minutes, and then meet her in room 815. When he gets there, she's already naked, waiting under the king bed's sheets. As she parts her legs for him, Eric looks over to the mirror-fronted closet door, and once again watches Solanum in his place, writhing on top of her, and he wonders if this is what it feels like to be consumed by the color.

ERIC HAS SEEN dozens of photos and hundreds of hours'

worth of video of Nasrin Addai, Solanum's former pilot. He knows the reason she can't pilot anymore is due to a spinal injury she received in the field long before Eric took over her Instar. So what he expects when he meets her, he's ashamed to say, is an invalid, and all the prejudices that come with that word he shouldn't have thought. But when the door to Nasrin Addai's apartment opens, he forgets everything he thought he knew.

She's beautiful in a sharp way, her brown skin not quite as dark as Eric's, her face laced by a few dignified wrinkles. Long, silver hair, and bright green eyes. A well-tailored suit over defined muscle, and a bust that makes the buttons on her shirt strain. She's taller than him in her heels. The only hint of injury is the cane she leans ever-so-slightly on. She smiles at Eric, his BSS escorts, the cameraman that's supposed to take their pictures and disseminate them to the news and run them up the chain to the recruitment offices. The smile is plastered on, but Addai does a professional-enough job of hiding it, lighting up her eyes as well as her mouth.

"You must be him," she says, switching her cane to her left hand so she can shake Eric's right. "I've heard a lot about you."

The camera flashes obnoxiously as they shake hands. "Come inside."

Nasrin Addai's apartment is…not what Eric expected. Or maybe it is. Maybe it should've been. It's very spartan. Small, efficient. It's an open floorplan, with a kitchen and a closed door leading to what he presumes is the bedroom. There's a small breakfast nook and a sliding door to a balcony. There are no photos of family members or friends, anything that would point to a kind of personality for the home. He wonders if it's been decorated in advance, like show homes for potential buyers; so it seems like someone lives here, but not with enough detail to tell who that person actually is. On the wall in the breakfast nook, Nasrin

Addai's BSS uniform hangs in a frame, its chest covered in medals, and he realizes he doesn't actually know very much—anything at all, really—about Nasrin Addai the person, only Nasrin Addai the pilot.

He knows from her file that she joined the BSS straight out of high school, like himself. Gunning for the pilot program from the jump. He knows she defeated seven Imagos in seven separate engagements, and that her eighth engagement is what ended her piloting career. But those are statistics, a scoresheet, not things that tell him about her as a human being.

Addai pours Eric a mug of tea (both of them "candidly" photographed the entire time) and they move out to the balcony, where a couple comfortable exterior chairs sit. Addai's apartment complex is in a nice part of the city, and from her balcony they watch another apartment complex's rooftop pool, where children play. Eric can hear their squeals of delight, a lifeguard's whistle, the water splashing. He's never liked pools. He always wore a shirt to the pool as a child. Being shirtless made him feel exposed in a way the other boys his age didn't.

"You have kids?" Addai asks.

"What?"

She nods in the direction of the pool. "You're looking rather wistful."

"Oh," Eric says. "No."

"Scars?"

Eric turns away from the pool. This time Addai's smile is truly genuine. He doesn't know what he expected her to be like, but it wasn't someone this direct.

The BSS handlers and escorts and cameramen mill about within the apartment, busying themselves with nonsense in between photo bombardments. For a moment, Eric and Addai are unobserved. Addai props her cane beside her, and then untucks her shirt. She turns slightly away so that Eric can see a thick, ropy scar, perfectly straight, stretching up her spine. A surgical scar. It's old, no longer red and enflamed, instead like a small hill running up the length of her back.

"I never wanted to get into a pool after this," she says, tucking her shirt back in. "Water therapy was part of my PT. Even a one-piece wouldn't cover it, so I wore a shirt. I fell onto a subway entrance. One of those green fence things. But you probably already knew that."

Eric has seen the video, but he lets her tell the story nevertheless. He lets her be so much more than he expected.

"I got hit by this huge Imago, like a reptilian gorilla. Arms like…fucking redwoods, man, with these spines running down its forearms, its elbows. Like built-in knives. It jammed me and those spines went straight through Solanum, damaged the PiT, cracked the cockpit shell. A bit closer and it would have been punctured, killed me outright. I had to eject while another Instar took the Imago on, and the pod fell onto that damn fence." She mimes her own fall, and past the shield of comedy there is tragedy in her eyes. No tears, but there is a longing. "And there's more than just the one on my back."

A bizarre sort of envy fills Eric. At least her wound left a scar. Guilt follows soon after.

"I'm sorry that happened to you," he says, because he can't think of anything else.

"It's alright," Addai says.

It isn't, not really, but Eric thinks she means it.

"How's she looking these days?" she asks. "Did they fix her up right?"

"Like she never had a scratch," Eric says.

"Good," she says. "Good."

They sit in silence for a moment, listening to the city sounds. The pool across the street, the cars honking below, the whirl of wind between the buildings. The camera shutter goes off in the apartment behind them and Eric knows the photographer is catching some actual candid shots. He tenses.

"Just let them be," Addai says. "You get used to being watched."

"That sounds very unappealing."

"I didn't say it grows more appealing, I said you get used to it."

After awhile, she asks, "How's she treating you? Solanum."

"Oh." They've already crossed some invisible barrier together, so he decides to trust Addai. "I've done the simulator dozens of times," he tells her, slowly, "and that's one thing. But it's different, actually existing…inside her." He's not sure why, but right now it's strange to refer to Solanum as *her*. His skin both crawls and flushes.

"Weird not having a dick, huh?"

Eric flushes even brighter. He stammers, looking everywhere and anywhere except at Addai.

"Relax, kid," she laughs. "Everybody thinks about it, even if nobody actually talks about it. They feed you the company line, tell you about the dysphoria, but not in any way that matters because they don't understand it." She switches to a mocking tone, reciting verbatim lines Eric recalls from the pilot training videos and manuals. "'Instar pilots may feel instances of body dysmorphia during or after piloting. This is completely natural.' 'Pilots may develop an intense attachment to their Instar, and disassociate with their own body. This is completely natural.' Blah, blah, blah." She blows a raspberry, and the last bit of Eric's mental construct of Nasrin Addai shatters under the reality of her. "You may have noticed—in fact, I saw you noticing," she says, gesturing to her chest, "that I am a rather well-endowed lady."

"No, I didn't—"

She holds up a hand, smiling again. Again, genuinely.

"I said relax, kid. It's hard not to notice them. I considered breast reduction surgery when I was younger. Even then I was a D cup, and these girls are *heavy*. Of course everyone convinced me not to. Friends.

Boyfriends, of course. Even my mom. But, you know, when I stepped into Solanum I felt, literally," she laughs, "a weight taken off. It was weird, but it was also nice, to be free of them for a little bit. If only because it made my back hurt less. So, what I'm trying to say I guess is however you feel is okay, whether you think it's you or not. It may be you."

Later, Eric sifts through the pictures taken of the two of them. There are hundreds of variations: the two of them meeting, Addai pouring him tea, the two of them standing posed beneath Addai's uniform, overlooking the city.

But Eric finds himself drawn to one of the few actual candid shots: him and Addai sitting on the balcony, taken from behind. They're both cast in silhouette, heads turned slightly towards one another. It's intimate, private, and Eric requests a printout of that picture and only that one, a small version for him to keep in his pocket.

Eric and Cassandra lay tangled in the sheets of a hotel bed, sweaty and panting after their…what was it they did? It certainly wasn't lovemaking. It was a cruder word. Fucking? Perhaps. Their actions possessed the same animal, primal need as mating. Scratching and biting, grunting and thrusting, sweat-slicked and breathless. But procreation wasn't the goal, pleasure was.

But was it? Eric finds pleasure with her, but he still cannot sort out exactly what kind it is. Or why.

Eric wants to tell her about meeting with Addai, the things she told him. He wants to ask Cassandra about how her breasts feel when she's inside Lunatus, if their absence bothers her. And he might have, if not for the fact that immediately after Cassandra finishes, coaxing Eric to climax right after, she peels herself from astride him and announces she's got to shower, that she has an interview coming up later.

Eric sees himself out.

THE GIANT, HALF-COMPLETED skeleton sits in an enormous, aquarium-style water tank. But instead of water, the tank is filled to the brim with a thick, viscous goo the noxious green of cartoon boogers or radioactive waste. The soft tides of the goo ripple with a unique shimmer, like golden flakes of sand reflecting against the light; the amber, what makes all this possible. There's no musculature covering the skeleton yet, no skin; it hasn't grown in. Just tendons like bridge cables connecting bones the size of oak trees. The spine of the half-completed Instar juts downward, tapering off to a small point, where it swarms with insectoid drones the size of housecats, building the Instar piece by piece, lumbar by lumbar.

Eric stands outside the tank, at the head of a group of school-aged children on a tour of an Instar factory. They're in a large, bland hallway, standing before an enormous hole cut out of the wall to display the in-progress Instar. The actual factories aren't quite so picturesque, but this is a museum version, designed to show people how the Instars are made without actually getting them in the way of their creation. Earlier they'd passed an automated machine with a dozen arms, all of which moved in unison to piece together an automatic rifle the size of a schoolbus. The group passed display tanks that held samples of the amber in its solid, liquid, and gaseous states. They passed the preserved skulls and teeth and claws of Imagos that had been defeated in battles long past.

When Eric noticed this moment on his itinerary,

though he knew he was only expected to give brief speeches at select moments, the thought of standing up before a group of children made him even more nervous than standing before the crowd at his graduation. The kids were already assembled when he arrived, coming in through a side entrance, not making another spectacle of himself as he'd been forced to at the stadium. He wondered how many of them actually wanted to be there. He remembered his own adolescence, wondering when something would come along that would push him in a direction he'd always told he'd be pushed, or ignite the passion in him he was always told he'd find.

Would he be Darius Draven for any of these children? And why did that thought make him queasy?

Eric cranes his neck up at the Instar's skull. Human enough, rounded, with two sockets for eyes, though there is no mouth, just a flat plate of bone; there's no need for an Instar to eat. Eric remembered reading during his early pilot training that a few of the older model Instars did, in fact, have mouths, only they were not for eating, but had sharpened and filed teeth, and were to be used as weapons. Different Imagos had barbed tails, quills along their spines, teeth and claws, so why not give the Instars another weapon in addition to their swords and spears, axes and guns? The public hadn't liked that, and the pilots had liked it even less. One of Eric's textbooks contained a partially-redacted report about a pilot who washed out almost immediately after biting an Imago in combat, even though the move was only done out of pure desperation. The pilot was honorably discharged to receive mental health treatment.

Eric wonders what happened to him.

"And here," the tour guide says, pulling Eric back into the present moment, "is a view of the Instars assembly." She's another BSS agent, wearing an identical uniform to the one who gave Eric's graduating class their itineraries.

She explains the use of the amber in the Instars' creation, but also highlights the danger of the material, comparing it to all different kinds of fuel humanity has used throughout time; natural gasses, fossil fuels, nuclear power.

"But there is," the tour guide says, "someone who knows more about that than me. You've seen him on the edges of our group, but let me formally introduce to you all, Instar Pilot Eric Fisher!" The woman gestures to him and then begins clapping, egging the children on. They clap halfheartedly, as everyone who is forced to clap does, and Eric takes a half step forward, gives a similarly-halfhearted wave, and clears his throat, daunted by the sea of tiny faces.

"Hello, everyone." He's already forgotten what class they are, what school they come from. Some of the children seem distant, bored with this whole endeavor. Some of them are still distracted by the enormous skeleton looming above them. But others look at Eric wide-eyed, and he imagines that must be the way he stared at Darius Draven on the television, seeing someone just like him in a position of not just power, but glory.

What was he supposed to say again?

"The amber," Eric starts, hitches, trying to remember his lines, or at least the vague shape of them, "is what powers our Instars. But, uh, like your teacher said," he says, realizing this woman is not their teacher, but he keeps going, "it is also very dangerous. Which is why we have to handle it with care."

One child shouts out from somewhere in the crowd without raising his hand, "Is that really what turns people into monsters?"

"Imago," Eric corrects, looking for who asked the question but not finding him, simply addressing the room. "Yes, that's correct. If you handle the amber improperly, or if you get too much of it inside you, it can hurt you.

Just in the same way as you wouldn't want to spend too long near other fuel sources, like burning gasoline or coal or radioactive material. But with us pilots, our Instars protect us from the dangers of the amber. They control it in the right way."

"What if you get some on you?" a little girl with curly hair in the front row asks. She looks worried, as if one of those monsters could appear at any moment. "People say if you get some on you and you're sad, or you're angry, it could turn you into a monster."

"We have doctors for that," Eric says, trying to simply be reassuring. He doesn't tell them all the specific purging protocols or the blood-level readers the pilots have to go through during each disembark, how scientists all around the world were still looking into the exact mechanics of transformation. Was each person's threshold for how much of the amber can be inside them before they change different? Was it really linked to the psychology of a person? Was it something entirely beyond their control? He doesn't tell them about the mental tests pilots have to take, the detox techniques the BSS has developed, with varying degrees of success, the dozens of safety protocols and redundancies in place. He simplifies it all for them, the Imagos, his pilot training, his responsibilities now that he's no longer a cadet. He doesn't tell them about the mental tests he takes whenever he comes out of Solanum, doesn't tell them about the people with the Imago masks. He doesn't tell them how he feels when he's inside Solanum or about how he is starting to feel something inside him, rising within him.

Part of him thinks what he's doing isn't just a mere simplification for the sake of the children.

That part that accuses him of lying.

Eric slips out of the tour before it officially ends, heading outside through a side exit, into the cool twilight air.

Eric tells himself that wasn't the BSS back here feeding them lines—it was him. And maybe, for one of those kids, they'll think of him the way he thinks of Darius Draven. This thought, and the cool wind, almost brings him back to himself.

But at the end of the alley, as he turns the corner, there's a harsh, blinding light, and he's jolted right back out.

"**D**OWN! DOWN! GET down on the ground!"

Hands on him. Shoving him down.

Someone is screaming. His knees hit the pavement with a *crack!* that sends a jolt all the way up his legs and into his spine. Something hard and cold is shoved against the base of his skull.

A gun barrel.

He's going to get shot in the street.

Eric doesn't know how to speak. He doesn't know what to tell them, doesn't even know who they are. He doesn't know what excuse will be good enough. All he can do is stammer as voices yell all around. Heavily-booted feet thunder around him, swarming the building.

"I'm a pilot!"

A moment of silence as the barrel presses harder into Eric's skull.

"Don't fucking shoot me, I'm a pilot!"

The barrel's pressure recedes a bit. Then, that first voice, utterly horrified, says, "Oh, shit."

The barrel leaves the back of Eric's head. He's grabbed gingerly under his arms and hauled to his feet. Flyers on the walls, a dumpster, discarded trash, everything graffitied. The alley absolutely filled with people and light. All around him there are men in full body armor, including helmets, all their visors lowered so that they reflect only the glare of the head- and roof-lights from the huge trucks that have blocked off the alley in both directions. It takes a moment for Eric to realize most of the figures are looking in the same direction, and that it's not at him.

There's a woman on the ground to his left, maybe fifty feet away, at the mouth of the alley, silhouetted by the bright lights. She's on her knees, her hands zip-tied behind her back. Her long, dark hair obscures her brown face. Her body hitches up and down in irregular rhythms. She's sobbing. Desperation is coming off her in waves, her color flowing out of her and washing over the alley. Her terrible, soul-crushing resignation is palpable. This woman has been exposed to the amber, and it's pouring out of her. She must work at the factory, exposed, contaminated, even in this sterile, safe place. All that's left now is the mechanics of the change, the scales replacing skin. The men in body armor can't feel her the way he can; their suits, like the Instars, are insulated to keep any foreign colors out.

"What the hell's going on?" Eric asks the soldier who pulled him up. They know he's a pilot now, so he's tempted to try throwing his weight around. But he flinches at his own dark, harrowed face reflected in the soldier's visor—his status wouldn't be enough to offset who he was born as, what he looks like.

"Do you know this woman?" the soldier asks.

They're going to kill me. The thought is not his own. It's hers. He can see it in her eyes.

"No." Staring into that visor, at his own face, Eric knows he's not naked, but it feels like he is. Without the protection of Solanum's hull, Eric is just a bug, something that could get squashed by accident, completely wiped from the face of the world. From its memory, even. If something happens, there's nothing to protect him. Nothing but his own soft, squishy, malleable body. His body that is so vulnerable to knives, bullets, fists, teeth.

"Who are you?" the soldier asks.

"A pilot. I just graduated."

"Test him," a voice calls from somewhere behind the wall of light.

"But he's a pilot," someone else says. "We might not be able to tell."

As the soldiers talk amongst themselves, the woman watches him with wide, red-rimmed eyes through the curtain of her hair. Gold flickers in the blue of her irises, and there's a strange serenity in her expression despite tears streaming down her face. Like she knows her fate and has accepted it. Her left cheek is scraped from being slammed into the pavement. Her lip is split, and she only wears one shoe. Eric could ask her if she is alright, but that will only make everything worse.

One of the soldier prods Eric. "We're going to need to test you. Could you pull your collar down?"

He knows why, but obstinacy flares up inside him. "Why?"

Another soldier steps forward. Just a half step. His gun isn't raised, but he's holding it. Just like the others. "Pull your collar down."

Eric does what they ask, wondering if they'll be able to tell, if what's pouring out of the woman is affecting him at all. One of the soldiers presses the same device from the doctor's office, from his disembarkings, against Eric's neck. There's a single, sharp twinge, and then the soldier removes it. The device beeps once.

"Okay," he says, "You're good to go." He looks back at the other soldier. "Get him out of here."

The man reaches to grab Eric by the arm, but he shakes the soldier loose.

"Wait a moment. Tell me what's happening here. What has she done? She can't be a threat to anyone."

"That's none of your business," the lead soldier says.

"What are you going to do to her?" He suspects she'll be taken, disappeared. They'll experiment on her to learn more about the change.

The soldier repeats, emphasizing each word; "That's none of your business."

The soldier's expression is blocked by his visor, but it's clear the impassive man has had enough; he stands feet apart, weapon before him, making himself into a brick wall.

"You can leave here," he says, "or you can be removed from here. It's your choice."

Eric picks the path of most resistance.

ERIC KNOWS IT was stupid. And yet he did it anyway. And because of that stupidity, he finds himself sitting alongside a handful of other despondent men in a too-cramped holding cell. He imagines he won't be there for long—the commander of the troops who arrested him is already on the phone, trying to track down someone whose authority he believes.

Never mind that Eric is a *human being*, and shouldn't be treated this way.

But that's not the point. The point is the woman. The bright lights in the middle of the night. The cuffs they put around her wrists. The windowless van they hauled her off in. The needles and blood pressure cuffs and tweezers and experiments that awaited her. Eric's thoughts bounce around, unable to focus on anything but her, on that moment.

He still doesn't know what possessed him. He just snapped. A soldier made a move toward the woman, likely to haul her up, and Eric's combat training kicked in.

Then his memories became a whirl of fists, light glinting off armor, deep grunts and the *thud*s of batons and fists against his body, and Cassandra showing up out of nowhere, screaming for them to stop. She, of course, wasn't arrested, even though she argued with the officers the whole time Eric was being loaded into the van. She shouted, and then she cried. Eric felt a punch as hard as the officer's baton when, as the van's doors were being closed behind him, Cassandra's face turned simply impassive, like a switch had been flipped. The tear-streaks were still there, but her face was blank, as if she was suddenly bored. The waterworks didn't get her what she wanted, so she simply shut them off. Did she care? At all? Or were her tears just a tool in the same way those batons were?

Eric tells himself that he is not like them. No matter how he walks, how he talks. How he acts, how he dresses. Even though he is a pilot, he is still separate from them.

He never stood a chance in that fight. Not against that many men. Not when they were all armed. If he wasn't a pilot, they certainly would have killed him. But if he wasn't a pilot, would he have been brave enough to throw that punch? Did he only do it because he knew his uniform acted as a shield?

His thoughts drift again; the more he thinks about the fight, about his reasons for throwing the punch, the less it becomes about the soldiers who were standing there in front of him. Maybe there was another world where Eric did stand a chance. A world where he could have taken them. Freed the woman. Done something about her exposure to the amber. Saved the day. Been the person he wanted to be, the person they told him he could be, even though they lied.

Eric reaches up and touches his face, the wounds he received from an actual man-to-man battle. He hasn't been in a fistfight since he was in high school, since he saw Tommy Legretti beating up Norman Holt.

Eric didn't know the reason, didn't care, just jumped in to help Norman, the shy, quiet kid who tended to stay out of everyone's way. He won that fight against Tommy, and people treated him differently after that. Like he was dangerous. But he was ten.

With his adrenaline finally receding, Eric can feel his own rewards from what was less of a fight and much more of a beating; a punch to the face that was quickly swelling into a black eye. A bruised jaw. A split lip that's a single point of sharp heat among all the dull aches of all the blows his chest and shoulders, back and legs took.

But even with all of those fresh wounds, Eric still finds himself entranced by his left arm. His completely uninjured left arm. He keeps expecting to see something there. A cast. Scars. Stitches. *Anything.* But there's nothing. It makes perfect, logical sense that his Eric-injuries stay with him and not his Solanum ones. But feeling and logic are completely different beasts. If an injury is a punishment, a punishment against the flesh, then what else could these be, but punishments for inhabiting this form?

Hearing his name called keeps him from descending into a panic-spiral.

Loretta.

"Him!" she says as she charges into the hall outside the cell, ahead of a uniformed police officer. She's clearly at the end of a long night; bags under her bloodshot eyes, her sparse makeup noticeably runny, her blazer unbuttoned and floating behind her like wings. The sight of her face floods him with relief, just as her uniform pours unexpected acid into his veins. He thinks of Nasrin Addai's medal-adorned uniform hanging in its case on her wall, less like a badge of honor and more like a dark specter, always watching. He knows he'll never forget the way she looked at it. Such disdain. That disdain will stay with him, has already burned its way into him.

"That's my pilot!" Loretta shouts. "Get him out of there!"

A police officer begrudgingly opens the cage and waves Eric out. The rest of the men inside mournfully watch him go. They'll be free in the morning, he hopes. Loretta grabs him by the shoulder, says "I got it from here, chief," to the officer, and drags Eric out of the station.

When they're outside, things change. He expects her demeanor to shift, or maybe he just hopes for it, but she only turns the spotlight of her anger onto him, her glare a searing blast.

"That was fuckin' stupid." She waits until a dark SUV with Bureau of Special Services-branded plates pulls up to the curb, its electric motor hissing. Eric flinches, remembering the dark doors they tossed the woman into. The front window rolls down and Cassandra peers out. For a moment it seems like she's going to say something, but what is there for her to say? What can she possibly say, Eric thinks, that could quell this moment?

I knew *guys like you could fuck like that.*

Silently, Eric gets into the back of the SUV, and Loretta rides shotgun. They pull off into traffic, dropping Cassandra off at the hotel, then turning towards the *Daedalus*. Loretta doesn't need to explain how much trouble he's in.

They ride in silence for an excruciatingly long time until Eric finally speaks up. "Are you going to ask them to reassign me?"

"No." Her voice is flat. Monotone. She looks into the rear-view mirror at him. "I get it."

Eric thinks about his face reflected in the officers' helmets. The fists crashing down on him. The batons flying at his head and chest. The woman being loaded into the truck, impassively accepting her fate. He didn't stand a chance. He wonders how he's supposed to stand a chance when the thing he's fighting is not a thing, but an idea. He thinks of Nasrin's uniform, of the commercials and posters with Cassandra's face. He thinks about Darius

Draven spilling out into the world after his glorious victory, and how something that meant so much to him, that defined him, could also do such irreparable harm without him even knowing.

His body still aches from the blows of the nightsticks and Eric focuses on that pain, tries to hold it as tightly as he can.

Something inside him tells him he deserves it for allowing this all to happen.

WHEN ERIC GETS back to his room aboard the airship, he slams down onto his cot, lifts his head to his hands. He tries to hold on while the world continues to spin out of control.

I'm alone, he thinks—does he? Is it his voice?—*I'm in the dark.*

After Darius Draven had that moment on TV, Instar action figures were sold in every store. As a teenager, he read the man's autobiography, attended recruitment fairs, and was subjected to military propaganda in every single piece of media he saw. What were the choices he had, the decisions he faced? None of them ever really seemed like decisions at all, did they? Was this the only place he ever could have ended up, funneled through his entire life and straight into the military machine like any other piece of hardware? Did the world give him any other choice but to end up here?

That's all he is to them all. To Cassandra. To the military. The BSS's Instar program.

Just a body.

Just a tool to be used.

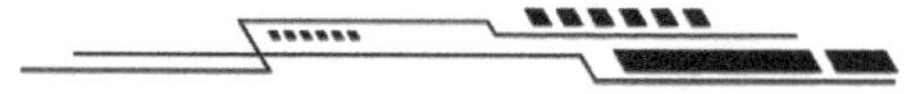

Unconsciousness finally takes him. At least for now.

In his dreams he's somewhere else. Someplace like the void, a mindscape, an endless nothingness, darkness spilling out forever, lit by occasional flashes of cosmic violet. In those flashes, Eric catches glimpses of his graduation, the cadets all clustered together, the shape of the auditorium lost in the darkness. Another flash: Nasrin Addai, eyes downcast from the framed uniform that hovers before her. The *Daedelus* and its underslung guns. The parallel lines of awaiting Instars. Darius Draven standing on the beach. Cassandra.

In this dream, he's someone else. He's not Eric. But he's not Solanum either. He's someone different.

He's someone new.

Dream-light comes from everywhere and nowhere. His naked, hourglass-shaped body is bathed in glistening white moonlight—not exactly his own, and not exactly Solanum's, but an entirely new entity. The lines and curves are smooth and sculpted. Deliberate. Purposeful. As if made from every single unconscious image Eric has ever imagined for himself and pasted together perfectly. His chest and face are hairless, not even the hint of stubble remaining inside the follicle when he shaves it down. There's only smooth, unblemished skin. His wedge-shaped torso is tapered at the waist, widened at the hips. When he lifts his arms in the moonlight, the muscle and fat deposits have been displaced and reorganized. Though they're not the arms he's used to, they're *his arms.* His crotch is featureless, replaced with the smooth curve of an action figure. The brown skin and lavender hull merge perfectly, a color he can't completely grasp within the dream—maybe it's a color that hasn't even been discovered yet. Whatever the color is, it's *his.* Like it's *him.,* like he's finally dropped the weight he's been carrying all his life. Is this what the Book of the Metamorphosis meant, about the amber providing a gift?

An orange lightning bolt flashes in the distance, but it's slower than the others, even in slow motion, revealing not a single image like before, but only the vague shape of something vast. Eric squints. Realizes it's not the lightning, but a light. A series of lights on the side of some enormous thing. It's far, far away, but that means little for its size. Eric knows it could be over to him in a moment. It's a darker shape among the rest of the darkness, until that orange flares and its edges light up. There's just enough for him to realize there's something there, but not what it is. It's orange light glinting off rows of scales, the edge of a massive, reptilian form.

SOLANUM

PART III

HATCHING

THE DOOR TO Eric's room opens after a perfunctory knock that's more warning of imminent entrance than expectant of an explicit invitation. Loretta stands in the doorway.

"Hey," she says, her voice scratchy. Like she's been yelling some more. "Making sure you're still alive."

A moment of silence.

"We didn't really get a chance to talk," she says, "after."

"What happened to her? That woman?"

Loretta says nothing. They both know. A black site. Under a microscope.

"Are *you* alright?"

"It's nothing that won't heal," Eric says. "Look, if you're here to reprimand me or tell me whatever consequences there will be, it's fine. I'll take them. Nobody made me punch those guys." He thinks about his life. About his decisions. About how, his whole life, it seems like something has been making him do things whether he's aware of it or not.

Something he's only been distantly aware of until recently. He wonders when it was, before that punch thrown at the soldiers, that he made a decision that was truly his own.

"There aren't going to be any consequences," she tells him. "Nothing serious. I'm supposed to be in here giving you a verbal warning."

"Just like that?" he asks, wondering how, wondering why. Is it because there are so few pilots now? Is it because they can't spare him? Is it because someone pulled strings? Is it because the BSS is supposed to take care of their own? No consequences.

"Just like that."

Eric doesn't know if he wants any part of that.

"You know what it's like when you're inside, when you're piloting?"

Loretta nods, her face making it clear she's unsure where this is going.

"You're you, but you're not really you."

"Yeah. Well…that's how I feel when I'm Eric. Everything is out of sync."

The wheels in Loretta's mind spin slower as she tries to sync up with him. "That fight," he continues, "it felt like… like what I imagine fighting in an Instar feels like. It wasn't real, almost. But being in Solanum makes it more real."

Eric can see the point where Loretta's brain overclocks. It's subtle, she's used to quelling her emotions, but her eyes still widen, her pupils still dilate.

"I know what you're thinking," he says, "But it's not the dysphoria the textbooks told me about. This is something different. When I talked to Addai, she told me about how her back felt better in an Imago because of…" Eric can't bring himself to finish that sentence in front of his mentor.

Loretta chuckles dryly. "Yeah, I know what she means. Look, if that's…" she stops and then starts again. "Only you know how you feel, right? And what do I always tell my pilots?"

"To trust your gut."

That's when the alarm goes off, sounding all Instar pilots to muster stations.

ALL AROUND HIM, pilots and technicians are falling out of their bunks and hurrying into their uniforms. There are hushed whispers that are attempts not to panic, but the fear can clearly be heard under the thin veneer. Boots stomp loudly down the hall, attempting the practiced rhythm of trained soldiers, but consistently breaking it, though it is unclear whether it is due to fear or clumsiness. For just a moment the alarm calms down and a voice comes in over the loudspeakers.

"Solanum, Lunatus, deploy. Brassica oversee."

Solanum, Brassica, and Lunatus. Eric, Loretta, and Cassandra. This is it, the moment he's been waiting for. After Fleet Week, after Nasrin Addai, after everything with the soldiers and the woman, all those horrible things piling up inside his brain, here is Eric's chance to escape it, at least for a little while. Here is his opportunity to flush all that away, to become who he felt he really ought to be. The mere thought of it sends a thrill through him.

But then there's Lunatus. The name that sours the rest of it. That's the name of Cassandra Vort's Instar. It's Lunatus' name that's enough to pull all those awful thoughts back into the foreground of Eric's mind. Cassandra. His body. Fleet Week. The photo shoot. Addai. The Instar floating in the tank. The soldiers. The woman.

This isn't how it was supposed to be. Eric always believed his first fight with an Imago would be thunderous, heroic. He thought it would be something people wrote songs and made movies about. Nothing like this. He wanted to be a hero, not shirking his duty for a fix of whatever bizarre addiction he seems to be developing when it comes to Solanum.

Now he just wants to be someone else.

HIS WHOLE LIFE, Eric has been told that boarding an Instar is a strange, often uncomfortable process. When anyone asks him, he agrees, because on the surface it should seem that way: being penetrated by a strange machine, submerging in a kind of amniotic goop. Eric knows he should find it more unsettling, but to him the whole process seems almost sensual.

Or at least it would on a good day, if everything were going right. He'd like to sit in it, the sharp feeling of the centipede sliding into his back, the warm cocooning inside the cockpit. Instead, Eric stands beneath the crouching Solanum, nervous about his nudity. He's so exposed. He is hyper aware of the hair on his chest, on his arms, of the tone of his muscles and the cock between his legs, even shortened in the cold. Aware of everyone watching him like a butterfly pinned beneath glass.

Biggs hands Eric his oxygen mask, and when he does, he assesses Eric's shoulders, his biceps. Not sensually, not alluringly, but maybe the way someone would look at a statue in a museum. Eric does his best to ignore it, takes the mask and slips it over his head.

"Ready?"

Eric nods. Standing under Solanum, everything else is suddenly erased. The thoughts of the soldiers and the woman and that drunk tank still play in his mind, but they're far, far in the background, drowned out by the physical presence of the Imago, of the thought that, in a moment, Eric will no longer entirely be Eric anymore. He'll be what he wants, who he wants, who he knows he was supposed to be, and everything will be easier to think about then. Won't it?

Biggs picks up the centipede device from where it dangles from the waiting Solanum's chest cavity. "You ready for this?"

"I'm ready," Eric says, turning his back to him and bending over, trying to shut out everything but this moment. He flinches as Biggs attaches the device, as dozens of acupuncture-thin needles penetrate him, burrowing down into his spine, connecting to his nerves. Eric's vision doubles, receiving visual data from the hangar through Solanum's eyes as well as his own. The broad back of Eric-body is hooked into the centipede below him, nearly prone, like a child spilled forth from the womb.

The egg-shaped cockpit lowers to the ground, and Biggs helps him step backwards into it, giving Eric a thumbs-up as the door closes. Eric shuts his eyes at the small warning noise that precedes the hatch opening above him. The gel comes pouring down, a familiar spill over his head and across his body. A pleasant warmth spreads over his body, as if he's sliding into a hot bath. Eric breathes through the oxygen mask as the gel rises up and over his head, until he is entirely submerged.

Through the gel, reflected against the door of the cylindrical cockpit, Eric catches a distortion of his face and body, warped by the glass and the liquid. A mask covers his nose and the bottom half of his face in a thick layer of plastic, its oxygen tube snaking up and away, into the same tube above him the wires from the centipede disappear into. His eyes are intense. Warm. Biggs throws the switch that pushes Eric's body away, replacing it all with Solanum. She's everything he wants to feel, everything he's been *terrified* of feeling, everything he knows he can't run from even before he knew he was running. He doesn't want to run from it anymore. He needs to embrace it. If he doesn't, he'll simply perish. Solanum's flesh isn't cold metal, it's warmer than his own with the cosmic color flowing through it, warmer than anything he's ever felt.

Like it was made for him. This is the existence he's been waiting for, that's he's denied himself his entire life. Solanum's broad shoulders and slender waist, her wide hips, the absence of anything between his legs—he knows the name of that feeling now, connecting with the Instar.

It's euphoria.

THE MASSIVE FREIGHT elevator carries Solanum and Brassica up to *Daedalus'* upper deck. The elevator is enormous, set against the rear of the hangar, and through the chain link guardrail, Eric can look down on the rest of the hangar, and all the movement there. The technicians working on benched Instars and fighter jets. Bays of screens displaying battle information.

In the elevator, Brassica stretches the way Loretta usually does before a battle: she leans to the left and right, flexing her calves. Pulls her arms up and behind her. Bends over, touches her toes. Eric is fascinated by the whole thing. Is there a point to it? People don't stretch out their swords and knives. And yet Instars have muscle and bone and flesh and arteries just like people.

He mimics her, and begins to notice the difference even inside Solanum. Not the chill of hard metal, but the response of warm muscle, biomechanical tendons.

He thinks maybe there should be the sensation of
electricity as the cosmic color runs through the hull,
but instead there's a warmth that reminds him of hot
chocolate on a cold night. Stretching eases him into that
bigger feeling, of waking up from a long rest.

A long rest where he was stuck as just Eric.

Does Loretta feel this way? Does she feel as connected
to Brassica as he does to Solanum?

Eric doesn't think he can ask her. At least not yet. Not
with everyone else around. Truth be told, he doesn't even
know if he knows Loretta well enough for that question.
They shared a moment together in his room, something
she clearly sympathized with, but she's his trainer. They
know each other well. But are they really *friends*? Could
someone like Cassandra fill such a role after the strange
intimacies they've shared? He can't be sure. Eric pulls
all these questions back in before they get out, a sense
of shame lowering over him like a cold, wet blanket. He
imagines someone about to be waterboarded, the wet rag
laid over an indiscernible face, puffing in and out with
frantic breaths.

He remembers that woman in the alley down on her
knees, looking up at him through her curtain of hair with
that one, unblinking, accusing eye.

Above the Instars, a huge door opens, cold air rushing
into the shaft as Eric and Loretta ascend onto the top
deck. The air would normally be too thin, but he takes a
long, deep breath through Solanum and it seems like this
is how air is supposed to be, what it's supposed to taste
like.

Another freight elevator door opens up and Eric spies
Lunatus emerge. Cassandra's Instar is a slim, light model,
like Solanum, painted with a brown base, accentuated by
splashes of bright, fire-engine red. A long, thin sword is
slung across her back, and sharp studs are molded directly
into her knuckles.

Eric wishes he could read something, anything, on Lunatus' face. He doesn't know whyCassandra's expression is suddenly so important. He barely knows her. Or maybe it's more like he only knows one version of her. Even though he spent the last week with her. Even though they've slept together. Nevertheless, he longs for that comforting version of Cassandra, the one who eased his mind during the photoshoot. The hotshot pilot who knew everything would be alright because she succeeded at everything.

But Lunatus's face remains impassive.

Cassandra's voice comes in over the comms, sounding as if she's right next to him. "Hope you're not afraid of heights," she says.

Eric steps right up to the edge.

Frigid wind whips at his face and howls in his ears, unobstructed by buildings or nature, shrieking off the smooth surface of the *Daedalus*. Looking down, he thinks his stomach might drop out from beneath him. The *Daedalus* has reached its position above the city, is slowly lowering into the safe-to-drop zone, where the Instars will be able to leap off the edge into the battle below. From this high up, much is obscured. There's an Imago down there somewhere. But whatever and wherever it is, it's obscured by the clouds, the smoke, the sunlight glinting off the skyscrapers. Cassandra cracks Lunatus's knuckles. "Who's ready to thrash this thing?"

"No hotshot antics, you got me?" Loretta says in the voice of the commander, the voice Eric recognizes. "The second we leave this deck, I'm in charge."

A beat, and Eric wonders what's going through Cassandra's mind. Are things different now, now that they're real? The impassive face of Lunatus shows nothing.

"*Yes, ma'am,*" Loretta prods, and the two of them echo her. "Good."

Loretta joins Eric at the edge of the deck. "Brassica in position."

Smoke rises from the city below. "Solanum in position," Eric says.

"Lunatus in position." There is no crack in Cassandra's voice.

The control tower in their ears: "Deploy."

Once Solanum steps from the edge of the *Daedalus*, Eric knows they're falling, but for a moment, hanging there in the air, he's weightless. One beautiful moment where everything that has been holding him down is not just lifted from his shoulders, but erased from existence entirely. Nothing else matters but the wind on his skin, its fingers tickling Solanum's body—*his* body— the city rushing up to meet him.

This is how it's supposed to be, Eric thinks. This is what he's been missing for so long. A sense of *feeling*. The push and pull of the wind, the cold of the air, the pressure of gravity.

Is this it? Eric wonders. *Is this how people feel all the time?*

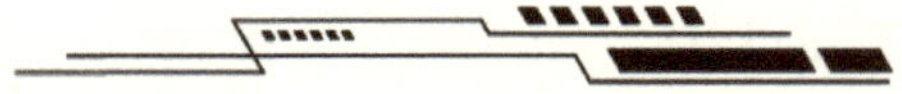

THE BEAUTY FADES. The city roars closer and he can pick out details of its destruction.

Even though Eric can only see the tops of most buildings, he can't miss the smoldering wound carved through the middle of the city, the trail of destruction a bright yellow-orange S. Like a venomous animal. Plumes of smoke rise up from that fiery trail, and the falling Instars try their best to angle out of its path. As they get closer, the shapes of landmarks and cars and people coalesce, and Eric's heart begins to jackhammer with fear, not just adrenaline.

To his right, Brassica and Lunatus barrel towards the ground, their mechanical faces impassive, stoic. Inside, are Loretta and Cassandra going through the same things he is?

Are they as nervous as he is inside their cockpits, sweat comingling with the gel swaddling them?

"Deploying chutes," someone from the *Daedalus* tower says in Eric's ear, their voice deliberately staticky to let the pilots know it's coming from the airship, to preserve their sense of orientation. He braces himself as the massive sets of parachutes installed onto Solanum's back deploy. A lurching against his chest as he decelerates. The chutes are huge, military-grade, initially developed to airdrop tanks into battlefields. And yet the Instar is bigger. Eric hits Solanum's thrusters to add to his deceleration, but nevertheless comes to an earth-shaking stop in the middle of an already-ruined street, blessedly clear of civilians. He sees her, a lavender blur reflected in the buildings as he pulls her limbs in, keeping them from taking chunks out of the sides. The lines on the parachute disengage and it snaps away, twirling off into the wind.

The tower says, "Solanum has landed."

Somewhere off to his right, Eric hears another thunderous *boom* and the quake reverberates up his ankles.

"Brassica has landed."

One more behind and to his left.

"Lunatus, landed."

As Eric brings Solanum to her full height, he comes level with a group of civilians on the fourth floor of what appears to be an office building, judging by the conference room that's had its exterior wall blasted entirely away. The civilians are visibly shaking and afraid, huddling together against the far wall of the conference room despite the door blown off its hinges, allowing their escape. Even when Eric tells them, voice booming out from the Instar's exterior speakers, that it'll be alright, they still turn and run. Back out on the street, cars and buses are scattered around Solanum's feet like childrens' toys. People running like action figures come to life. A few look up at him with relief, but most scatter with fear, like those in the office building.

Perhaps this is another reason why Instars weren't even more massive constructs: to help the pilots themselves remember. At this size, he can still hear and see all the people below and around him.

He hangs on to that, the thought of the people. He jettisons the rest.

There are people in trouble.

And the only ones who can protect them are Eric and his fellow pilots.

It's for them that he charges into battle.

THE IMAGO HAVE been appearing ever since the discovery of the cosmic color. The first transformation happened soon after miners started harvesting this exotic element as a possible fuel source. In school, Eric was taught that their transformations were disasters caused by improper handling, and prompted the protocols and procedures needed in every city for evacuation routes in the case of an Imago appearance. Eric remembers practicing many of those routines, the instructions given by his teachers and parents on where to go and what to do during the appearance of an Imago. Everyone was meant to shelter in place, whether it be in a rooftop sanctuary or an underground bunker. But most people didn't have places that secure available—he remembers hiding under his desk at school, wondering how a wooden desk would protect him if one of them decided to smash into the building.

There were always casualties.

"Just end it fast," Loretta says over the comms. "Nothing fancy." Eric remembers the rest of the lesson she gave him during training: The longer a battle goes on, the more collateral damage there will be. *I don't give a shit about property damage, but there's almost always people in property.*

Luckily, there are protocols for that too.

Few bystanders are left in the Imago's wake, but Eric still activates Solanum's onboard warning system: swirling red lights and a blaring alarm. Military-grade drones zip ahead of them, controlled by a whole team of scientists aboard the *Daedalus* whose only job it is to project the Imago's movement through the city and clear a path.

Eric directs Solanum into action, still watching her feet, moving lithely and gracefully through the city, following the Imago's path of destruction with his own senses, his direction confirmed by the signature locked into Solanum's computer. As the Instars approach from different directions, the ground quakes with their collective footsteps, the streets carpeted with shattered glass. Brassica's heavier steps put her somewhere to Eric's right, beside a bank. Somewhere behind him is Lunatus. Solanum picks up speed. Whips around a corner.

That's when he sees it.

And he's not ready.

EVERY IMAGO IS different. An endless, unrepeating stream of shapes and colors, but primarily insectoid, reptilian, and deep sea forms. Things that are as far away from mammalian, from human, as possible. These are what Eric believes has always defined Imago physiology.

But the one before him is something he's never seen before.

The Imago is a little taller than Solanum, almost five stories. A lithe, serpentine body tapers into a long, rudder-like tail spooling out into the city, knocking aside cars. It's bipedal, stumbling almost drunkenly forward on two stout legs while its arms pull it along the sides of buildings, knocking street signs and traffic lights from its path, tearing chunks of metal and concrete and glass from the buildings. It's brightly-colored, banded in red, black, and yellow, an asymmetrical speckled pattern dots its hide like vitiligo.

And then it turns, and Eric realizes this one's transformation is not yet complete.

The Imago is still partially human.

Its snout stretches forward, like it's trying to become something crocodilian but has stopped halfway through. That mouth is filled with mismatched teeth that can't decide if they want to belong to a predator or an omnivore, some carnivore-sharp, others grinding molars. None are in their proper place inside the mouth itself. That speckle pattern on its hide is human skin that has not yet been consumed and covered by scales. Patches of hair continue to fall out of its head. The Imago breathes and exhales a yellow-gold mist from its pores, its own personal color swirling lightly in the air around it.

Its eyes are wide and panicked. Not the doll-black of a shark, but terribly human, and bulging with fear.

"Stay focused." Loretta sounds just as shocked as Eric feels. His knees wobble, panic boiling through his veins. Eric tries to tell himself that whoever Imagos were before they transformed is gone, just like in the movies he watched as a child about zombies or extraterrestrial body-snatchers. He and the other pilots are here to deliver mercy, here to save those who still have lives left to save. He has to think of it that way, or else he's not going to be able to get through this.

But when he meets the creature's eyes, he doesn't know if he can. And judging by Loretta's voice, he doesn't know if she'll be able to either.

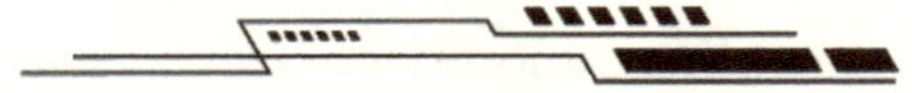

THERE ARE NO higher thoughts anymore, only sensations. No worries about the thought of what happened if you were mad or sad when you touched the amber, about the thing it could turn you—has turned her—into. No human left on the surface at all, just animal. Not the letters R-U-N, but merely the thought of run. There are threats before her, and she knows she cannot be there.

So she turns.

She runs.

Even though her bones are breaking, reforming as she moves. Her face and jaw is expanding, mouth turning into a snout. Snapping. Shifting. Replacing. Scales crawl all over her body, that yellow-gold surrounding her, inhaling her. It wasn't supposed to be like this. It wasn't supposed to hurt this much.

She wants her mother, but she knows she is gone, taken.

All that's left are the monsters.

The ones that are coming for her.

THE INSTARS RUN through the thinned-out streets, watching their feet as bystanders flee from their path. The local police have already done a decent job of clearing the streets, but Eric still keeps an eye out. The Instars follow as the Imago makes a beeline across the city, swimming through metal and concrete, thrashing at buildings. When it reaches the middle of an intersection, the Imago stops and thrashes aimlessly, its flailing limbs smashing and flinging cars. It spins in place as if it doesn't entirely know what it's doing or where it's going.

Neither does Eric. He wonders if the fear, this panic, is his alone.

"What do we do?" he asks Loretta as Brassica takes the lead. Cassandra is quiet on the line. "Have you ever seen anything like this before?"

Loretta is quiet for too long before she says, "Not in person."

Communication from the tower comes through to all of them: "Instars, you are clear to engage and neutralize the target." Of course they are listening up there in the *Daedalus*, reading the pilots' vital signs as well as tapping into their communications.

The Instars slow as they approach the Imago, catching a full view of its distorted form as they approach it from different angles. It still thrashes at nothing whatsoever. Not a building, not at the police who occasionally hope their pistols will do anything other than piss it off, but as if the air itself is attacking it.

"Jesus Christ, what's it doing?" Cassandra asks, getting a good look at the Imago for the first time.

"It's still transforming," Eric says.

A yellow gas roils off the Imago, scales climbing over the patches of human skin that remain, locking whoever this poor person was into this new form. The Imago's pupils stretch, as if pulled by invisible strings on either end into long, thin, reptilian slits. Barbs sprout the length of its spine, from the back of its head down to its rudder-like tail. Its already-existing claws lengthen, tearing canyons into the concrete. Finally, when it seems like the worst is over, the Imago stands, revealing its glorious, hideous new form. Taller than the Instars. Taller than the buildings. The Imago roars, shattering every pane of glass on the block.

And charges.

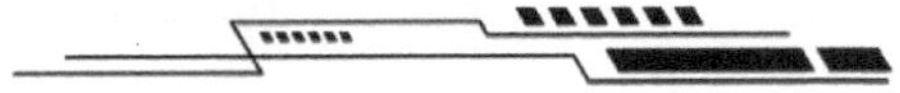

THERE IS SO little of her left now. She is almost gone. All of it eaten by the sadness that grew inside her when she touched the amber. She is without a name. Without a past. If it is there, it's buried somewhere distant. Deep. Buried with the memories of her mother and those men taking her away.

All she's aware of is being in danger.

Of having to fight for her life.

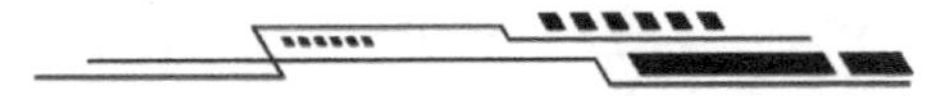

"You are clear to engage!"

Eric can hear the orders from *Daedalus*, but they bounce impotently off his skull. He doesn't really know what they mean. Everything he's seen over the past week, and now this? No, it's all just too much. He doesn't think he can handle it. In fact, he *knows* he can't handle it. Eric tries to think about how he could excuse just simply ejecting. Getting out. Running away and leaving all of this behind him. But he's coming up with nothing. Because of course he is. What he's imagining is going AWOL, and if he did that they'd come for him with the same ferocity as he's supposed to be coming for the Imago, this *person*, before him.

"Engaging!"

Someone screams and slams into Solanum. She staggers, collapsing on top of a convenience store. She slams down onto the roof, her knee taking out the front entrance as Lunatus shoots past him, charging the Imago headlong. Cassandra's cosmic color leaves a fingerprint across the gray matter of Eric's brain, telling him exactly what she is thinking: the Imago no longer looks human. The ambiguity and confusion have gone away and this monster is a safe target now.

"Lunatus, slow down!" Loretta screams over the com, but Cassandra is having none of it. Lunatus is a blur charging right at the Imago, her shortsword raised.

Somewhere, it seems like far away, Loretta yells "Be smart about this!"

Lunatus begins to unleash a huge, overhead swing with the sword. It's a wildly sloppy attack for someone as proficient as Cassandra, an attack anyone can see coming from a mile away.

The Imago certainly does.

It spins, quickly. Faster than a creature of that size should be able to move. Sweeping its tail around. The rudder knocks cars and buses aside. Its gravity rends canyons in the concrete. It knocks Lunatus' feet out from under her, stomps on her chest and digs its claws into her hull.

Cassandra's scream bleeds through the comms, a horrible, high-pitched wail. Glowing green fluid, her color, leaks thicker than blood from Lunatus' hull where the Imago's claws rent her side.

"Move!" Loretta's voice snaps Eric out of it as Brassica blasts forward. "Solanum, distract it. I'll retrieve Lunatus."

Eric has no idea what's going on between him and Cassandra. He doesn't know if they're simply copilots, if they're acquaintances, lovers, friends, whatever. But he does know running into danger to protect someone is easier than running into battle in order to hurt someone else.

Lunatus slaps feebly against the Imago's leg, the sword completely forgotten. Gone who knows where. Her initial scream crawls away and dies, rotting into a dull groan as her limbs impotently flap.

"Flank it!" Loretta shouts.

Eric obeys, Solanum breaking left, Brassica right, dividing the Imago's attention. Eric knew how much taller the Imago was than the Instars, but it's a completely different, terrifying thing to experience this close. The Imago turns its attention towards Brassica, and Solanum lunges, grabbing it by the tail. Pulling as Brassica pushes, staggering it. None of them are prepared for the horrible ripping sound they hear as the claws are pulled from Lunatus' hull. Cassandra's scream echoes as her color splashes onto the street. How much can she lose?

"I've got her!" Loretta calls as she hauls Lunatus to her feet.

Solanum and the Imago are caught in a tangle of thrashing limbs. They stumble across the street in an awkward dance, stepping on abandoned cars, triggering alarm after alarm. Solanum is pushed off balance and they go falling over together, the Imago landing on top of him, knocking the wind out of his lungs.

THOUGHTS COMING IN strange. Jagged. One thing's clear. She's in danger. She wants her mother. One thing's clear. She's fighting. She wants her mother. She doesn't want to fight. Doesn't like fighting. She doesn't want to hurt and she doesn't want to be hurt. The color amplifies everything inside her.

Somewhere out there, there's someone else who doesn't want to fight either. Just like her.

She—who is she? she forgets her name still—reaches out not with her hands because those have become claws, but with her mind. The only thing she has left. Taking the color and turning it. Using it. That tiny little sliver of it. Showing the last part of her.

Reaches out before it's completely gone.

LOSING THE AIR from your lungs isn't like people tell you it is. It isn't like the movies where everything slows down and blurs. Blind, panic claws at him as he tries to gasp for air. Eric's mouth moves, lips gaping, even though Solanum doesn't have them. He scrambles to get away from the thrashing Imago, clambering over splinters of rebar and the jab of hunks of concrete as he fights for purchase.

There's no one, singular moment where he gets air again. He draws it in slowly instead, a little bit at a time, as he kicks himself free from the tangle. Becomes more aware of the asymmetrical earthquake sounds of Instar feet rushing in, Lunatus groaning in pain somewhere far away, a nearby struggle.

Brassica grapples with the Imago, the creature flailing aimlessly, ripping, tearing, screaming, the Instar struggling to contain it in what little way she can, but it's only a matter of time until she falls. Her opponent is larger, more ferocious, fighting not with rage, but with desperation that's much more dangerous. The whites of the Imago's eyes, round and fear-bulged, spew a golden mist from every orifice, every pore. It thrashes, flinging that mist the length of the block, like a shower of spores catching the sunlight.

Eric gets an idea.

Somewhere, distantly, someone is yelling on the comm. But he ignores them. Instead, he stands up on wobbling legs. Lunatus leans against an apartment building to his right, its fire escape dangling precariously above her shoulder. Green flows from a gaping wound in her chest. Lunatus has no expressions on her face, but it isn't hard for Eric to imagine pain there.

"It'll be alright," he says. "Nobody has to die."

He turns away and wants to charge toward the tangled mass of Brassica and the Imago, but instead he gathers his mind, diving headlong through that golden mist spewing forth from the Imago, breathing it in, exhaling his own lavender, intertwining it with the gold just like with Loretta in the void before they were connected to their Instars.

Across their connected color, their communication moves as fast as thought, and their consciousnesses are somewhere else.

Sunspots dot Eric's eyes amidst a vast, endless blue. The surface of the ocean churns far above, sunlight refracting through water, lighting the seabed in a soft, comforting gloom. Twisting seaweed and sand drifting on currents surrounds him, and sparks of his lavender crackle through the water, lighting him and everything else in a soft blue-purple.

He's in the mindscape, that shared space, and he's alone. He's clothed this time, a simple pair of shorts and a T-shirt, almost long enough to be a dress.

"Hello?" he calls out to the empty ocean bed.

In the distance, something moves, a vast and hulking shape. Bioluminescence ripples across its hide. As the shape comes closer, its size warps as distance closes, making it difficult for Eric to figure out exactly how close it is. Soft jets of the cosmic color shoot out of the Imago's pores and into the mind-ocean as the creature swims toward him, a cloud that swallows it entirely. Eric doesn't prepare to fight. He doesn't retreat. He waits as the shape inside that cloud shrinks, and soon he finds not a monster, but a little Black girl in a tattered dress swimming toward him.

She's tiny, no more than ten years old, with the wild, unbound curls Eric once had as a child, before the world demanded he cut them. She approaches with the same inexplicable gravity that holds Eric to the bottom of this ocean, and sets her feet down on the sandy floor.

"I…I know you," she says, looking up at him. "Don't I know you? You seem familiar. But…like you're from a dream. Your colors are so soft. I thought…" She looks down. "I thought you might've been my mom."

"No," Eric says. "But I know you too." He is absolutely sure of it.

She's the Imago, but that's not entirely it.

He recognizes her from the tour of the factory: the little girl who asked a question. "Is that what happened?" he asks, recalling it. "Did you get some of the amber on you?"

"I thought I could use it," the girl says. "I thought I could use it to get my mom back. But I guess I took too much of it. Or maybe I was too sad and angry. I think that's how it changes you, because I didn't touch that much."

Jesus. The things this kid's been through.

"I'm Eric. What's your name?"

"Mina," the girl says, after a long pause. "Wilhelmina." She sits down on a nearby rock.

"That's a pretty name."

"I'm not pretty anymore," Mina says. "Are you going to hurt me like they hurt my mother?"

"No." Saying it aloud solidifies it for him. He knows, then and there, that he'll allow no harm to come to this Mina, Imago or not. There has to be some other way to solve this.

"No," Eric says again, "I'm not going to hurt you. And I'm not going to let anyone else hurt you."

Mina smiles, soft and small, but when Eric smiles alongside her, hers widens. Trust blooms in her eyes.

"We're safe down here in your ocean. For a little while anyway," Eric says. He knows it won't last long, that up above things are still moving, albeit at an infinitesimally-slow pace. Inside the mindscape they move at the speed of thought, but they can't stay down there forever. Maybe long enough to buy Eric some time to think of a real plan.

"I like to imagine the ocean when I need to think." Mina is quiet, and Eric can sense she has more to say, so he waits. She shrugs. "My mother told me about people throwing themselves into the ocean. A long, long time ago. Rather than be slaves. I always thought…it would be quiet down here. That there would be…people like me."

What on earth is he supposed to say to that?

"Do you…" Mina sniffles. "Do you know how to fix me?"

Eric's smile fades. "I don't," he says, choosing honesty. Not knowing if it's the right choice but choosing it all the same. "I'm sorry, I don't. Not right now anyway. But I do know I'm gonna do everything I can to try."

He offers her a hand.

Mina hesitates. "But what if I hurt somebody?"

"The only people we hurt this way is ourselves." The epiphany graces his lips before his mind even fully processes it.

Mina thinks about it for a moment, and then takes Eric's hand. He pulls her to her feet, and watches the smile flicker on her face as she's distracted by something over his shoulder. Eric turns, following her line of sight.

Cassandra is there. Without fanfare or announcement. She's struggling to hold herself up in her BSS uniform, which swirls in the mind-ocean around her, surrounded by the green of her cosmic color. She holds her chest where Imago-Mina tore into her.

"How did you get here?" Eric asks, shuffling in front of Mina. He asks the question without fully even realizing how *he* got there. He'd moved on instinct, on a guess, on luck. And it worked.

"I'm the best pilot in our class, remember?" Cassandra asks. There's a groan in her voice that slowly begins to recede as she realizes she didn't bring her wounds with her to this place, that she can relax. "You don't think I could figure out what happened after I saw what you did? What are *you* doing here?" She glares past Eric to Mina. "Why are you protecting her?" There's a growl in her voice, but even Eric can tell it's forced.

Eric holds up his hands, palms out in a surrender gesture.

"She called to me," he says. Mina huddles behind him. "She didn't mean to do any of this."

"But she still did it," Cassandra growls, still touching her chest like she took the wound personally. Eric knows how hard it is to let go. "People are still dead."

"She's just a kid." He doesn't know what there is between him and Cassandra—*it's just a little sport fuck between friends*—but he knows there can't be nothing. All the time they spent together has to mean something. "Cassandra," he pleads.

"So, what's your plan then?" she asks. She's not standing down. There's blood in the water, her blood, and she wants a fight. She wants payback. The last hit. Her emotions are rolling off her, her green color coming off her in waves, washing over his mind. This is what she trained for. This is what she gave blood, sweat, and tears for. She'd broken her back to be not just a pilot, but to be the *best* pilot. And here he was, demanding she stop?

"What are we gonna do?" she asks again, louder. "Are we gonna build a big Imago jail and keep her in there? Are we gonna spend all our time slapping handcuffs on monsters?"

"Maybe there's a way to turn her back," Eric says. "A detox?"

Cassandra laughs, and it's a dry, rotten noise.

"There has to be another way."

"Why did you join up, Fisher? You're here to fight. To be a hero. What would Darius Draven do? "

The question burns. He thinks about someone who looked just like him emerging from an Instar on the Golden Gate Bridge. Everything that came after: the action figures and the posters and the academy All because of Darius Draven.

But when he thinks of that moment now, he thinks of Mina. Of how this could be *her* Darius Draven moment. Someone like her is standing by, and will do the right thing. Whatever Eric does now, in the next moment, will mean everything to Mina. And everything to him.

"In here she's not hurting anyone," Eric says. "People are safe as long as we're in here." It's no solution and he knows it, but maybe it'll buy him time.

Cassandra scoffs. "We can't stay here forever. We leave the mindscape and then what happens? She becomes a monster again."

"In here we at least have some time to think," Eric says. "We can come up with a solution if we just do it together." He has no idea what that solution might be, only that he needs Cassandra on his side for whatever it is, and he can feel himself being pushed to the back foot.

The next few movements happen slowly. Almost imperceptibly. But they feel tectonic. Nothing moves on their faces; Cassandra steps closer, her color swirling around her, gaze narrowing. Mina shrinks even further behind Eric. Eric slowly squares up.

"Cassandra. Don't do this."

"I'm sorry," she says, "but we have to. It's what we were made for."

And then something like lightning strikes him right in the center of his back, setting every nerve ending aflame.

ERIC SCREAMS. HE tries to reach whatever has stabbed him but he can't. He's in so much pain, he's unsure of what body he's even in anymore. His muscles boil and his skin lights on fire. Somewhere in the distance a chorus of voices calls for him, asking what's wrong: Loretta's, Mina's, the voices from the *Daedelus*, all smashing together. He feels the hot city air on Solanum's skin, but also the warmth of the gel inside the cockpit, and he knows what's happened, if not how.

His connection is severed. The PiT, the centipede connecting him and Solanum, something is wrong with it.

Eric turns, moving the Instar's body as well as his own in the gel, trying to focus on one or the other but ending up on neither.

"Losing connection," someone says, and as Solanum falls, Eric catches sight of his—her—*their* reflection in a building, enough to see the Imago's–one of Mina's–long claw sticking out of his back, its wrist held by Lunatus' hands. Eric is shook—Cassandra brandished the body of the Imago itself as a weapon. Her impassive face says nothing, lets go of the claws. Nearby, Brassica gets up from where she had been thrown to re-engage the Imago, but she might as well be a million miles away. Loretta hasn't seen this betrayal.

"Solanum is hit," Cassandra says. Lunatus steps away from Solanum and tackles the Imago, pulling her away from the Instars. The claws slide out of Solanum's back with a slicing motion just as terrible as when it first entered.

Cassandra shouts, "Brassica, help him!"

Eric loses even more connection, the visual feed of the city street fading. The pulsing yellow of the pilot gel is turning to a horrid red. Catastrophic failure. He knows what comes next.

I can't, Eric thinks. He can't do it. Any of it. Can't separate. Can't be Eric again. Can't leave Mina alone, outnumbered. He promised. He swore.

But he has to.

He doesn't have a choice.

Against his own will, he ejects, spewing his fragile body out into the world.

IT'S LIKE BEING born again.

Eric goes flying out of Solanum, the Instar's eject sequence shooting him and the cockpit out of her stomach. He hurtles haphazardly through the air, slowing as the parachutes deploy, knocked about inside as the airbags burst to life. He crashes into a pane of glass, hitting something hard on the other side. Then he comes to a grateful, painful stop. This part he'd simulated, but not the rest of the eject sequence:: gel spews forth from the fractured cockpit, amidst warning lights and sirens, followed by voices from the *Daedelus* telling him that rescue is on the way.

No, he thinks. *I can't let them take me.*

He's not done with this fight.

The other Instars still fight with the Imago, and it sounds like the whole world is coming down around him.

Mina. Eric tries to call out, but it's like there's glass in his throat. He can barely move. He manages to roll onto his side and orient himself through the curved glass of the cockpit. He's smashed his way in through the front doors of a convenience store; they're blown completely off their hinges.

Beyond the store entrance, he can see multiple pairs of brightly-colored legs as the Instars grapple. The earth shakes with their combat: the few remaining intact windows rattling, canned food and bags of chips and snacks vibrating straight off the shelves. Brassica comes closer to the store, having abandoned the shell of Solanum to search for Eric's ejected pod. Beyond her, Lunatus and Mina thrash in a tangle of limbs.

Cassandra. She's going to kill Mina—kill a *child*—if he doesn't stop her. Separated from the Instars' commlink, he can hear nothing of their conversation, can't hear what excuse Cassandra gave for what happened to Eric, can't hear if Loretta believed them or not.

Gotta get up there. Eric tries to get to his feet, scrambling at the cockpit's gel-slickened walls. Outside, punches and kicks land with tectonic crashes, claws scraping with tremendous screams.

Something enormous crashes into the side of the building, shaking it, raining dust and rancid pipe-water down onto Eric. It's Brassica's hand, bracing herself against the side of the store. She kneels down outside, huge expressionless head visible through the storefront at him.

"Fisher, are you alright?" Loretta's question blares out through the Instar's built-in speakers, but Brassica's face doesn't change, doesn't emote.

Eric pulls himself up to his knees. To his goddamn feet. He drags himself along the shelves, over to the convenience store counter, past the cash register and to the front door.

"Get me out there," he shouts up to Brassica. He should tell her that Cassandra betrayed him. But he doesn't.

"Stay there," Brassica orders. "Rescue is coming."

She turns away from him like it's already settled. But Eric isn't done here. Not even remotely. He leans naked against the doorway of the store as she rejoins the fight.

Solanum is just across the street. She's crouched on her knees, arms dangling limply at her side, stomach flayed open from his ejection. If Eric can just get across the street, if he can get back into Solanum, then he can help Loretta. He can help Mina. He can do something to de-escalate this.

"Hey, buddy," a voice calls from behind Eric, "are you alright?"

Several heads peek up from behind store shelves; people hiding from the battle. The one who spoke lifts his head a little higher, a skinny kid with a blue polo, apron, and little wisps of a mustache. Probably not even out of high school.

"Are you okay?" the kid asks.

Among the small crowd, there's an old Black man with a carton of milk still gripped tight in one hand, and at his knees is a little boy, no more than five or six. He's holding onto the old man's leg for dear life.

"Are *you* all alright?" Eric asks. This is his duty, to protect the people. He pulls himself up straighter, heedless of his wounds, heedless of his nudity.

Slowly, the faces nod their assent.

"Then stay under cover," Eric says, his voice unwavering, strong. "Rescue will be here soon."

He turns on his heel and heads out into the street, pushing through every ounce of pain. Everything hurts. He's not sure if he's temporarily broken or irreparably damaged, but it doesn't matter. If he can stay alive for the next few minutes, maybe his steadily-forming plan will work.

A loud, metallic roar approaches from above. Eric keeps moving, knowing he can't spare even a single second, as *Daedelus* circles lower over the city. Those underslung gun turrets all point towards the tangle of flailing limbs two blocks down. BSS's final option, if their Instars are defeated in battle, is for the *Daedelus* to unload on the Imago. It's happened before, and there will be far more collateral damage than just Mina if that happens.

Even more bystanders will die.

Spewing forth from the *Daedelus* is a group of smaller craft, making their way towards him. Rescue.

Eric limps across the street to where Solanum hunches on her knees, her stomach ripped open like a burst fruit, cords and color spilling out onto the concrete.

This is a dumb idea, Eric thinks, even as he reaches behind him, tearing the centipede loose from his back. Instead of the strange painful-pleasurable sensation disengaging usually gave him, the movement incites a wet burn, like pouring acid in his wounds. He tosses the device aside as he steps into the color spilling forth from Solanum. It's warm, inviting Eric into the mindscape even as he stands there in the street, unconnected to his Instar.

Here goes nothing.

Eric selects the biggest of the frayed wires dangling from Solanum's split gut.

And he bites down.

Power. Power blasts away the pain of all the cuts and bruises, eradicates any sensation other than complete bodily euphoria, that sensation he's been struggling to name all along. The color is inside him, surrounding him—he's made of it. Eric is lifted up off his feet by his own hands, by Solanum's hands, tethered to her once again. The rest of the aimlessly-thrashing tubes rise to meet him, and as he holds down onto the largest between his teeth, he takes the others in his hands, positioning them behind his back until the frayed wires begin working their way into his wounds, his pores, directly into his skin. In the absence of the centipede, they merge him directly with the Instar, making him more than just Solanum, more than just Eric, the who he's always been, even though he didn't realize it. The color flows through his whole being, as if lavender runs through his veins now instead of useless, outdated blood. This must be what nirvana feels like.

Eric still. *Him* for now, because while he's sure this form isn't who he's meant to be, who he's used to being will do. For now. It'll do while he does what he needs to. The color pumps its cosmic fuel through him, making him more than he ever was before, controlled by his surety of purpose, pushing the fear from his body.

When he's ready, he plugs back into the Instars' comms. Someone from the tower announces that the *Daedelus* is prepared to engage.

"Stand down!" Eric shouts, with newfound authority. Down the street, Brassica struggles to pull herself out of an office building that's coming down around her ears. Lunatus is on her back, the fight slowly going out of her, trying to protect her stomach with one arm as the Imago violently tears at her. Lunatus' other arm is raised towards the Imago, the blue of Cassandra's color swirling with gold, as she tries to siphon energy from the Imago, replace her own leaking color.

"Lunatus, your levels are reaching critical mass," someone from the *Daedelus* says into their ears. "Your amber readings are off the charts!"

"I can handle it!" Cassandra shouts even as the Imago rips and tears at her, but Eric knows she can't. There's too much of it, and she's too far gone. Fear and desperation, obedience and confusion tear at her, amplified by the color, warping her.

Eric clenches his fists and a wave of lavender fire grows around him. It pulsates around his torso, curling around him, growing bigger, until it envelops him like a cocoon. The color is doing more than just running through his blood now—it's changing him. Healing him. Metamorphosing him too. The air around him ripples, as if the universe itself catches its breath at the audacity of his change.

The universe should rejoice.

"Lunatus," he calls, strong, sure, steadfast. "I'm coming!"

"Eric!?" Cassandra gasps, and there's a small silence after she uses his first name. Eric knows he isn't the only one who can feel a sea change in those syllables. "Stay back, I can handle this!" But she can't and he knows it. Everyone knows it. Everyone except Cassandra. Drowning in her color, in Mina's color, Eric can see the change before she can. Lunatus's hull rips and cracks, cyan light pouring out of her, a blue-gold, an unstable combination of colors, going past the boiling point.

"Cassandra, stop it!" Eric shouts as Solanum ducks, lowering her shoulder into the frantically-swiping Mina. She is changing as well, her eyes more human now, not the doll-black of an attacking shark. Solanum pushes her away harmlessly. Below him, Lunatus' hull is fractured, bleeding blue-gold light. And beneath that light…

Scales.

"Eric," Cassandra gasps on a private line. "Eric, help me. I'm scared." Lunatus's hull crackles, reptilian musculature forming beneath, hatching from the shell of the Instar.

"I'm going to get you out of here," Eric says. He remembers Mina, then amends the thought: *I'm going to get you* both *out of here.*

Mina charges forward again, still in her blind rage, but Eric is enough to stop her now. He grasps at their respective colors, feeling them, pulling them all together again.

MINA IS IN the mindscape. Waiting for him. Just like Eric expected her to be.

"You came back," she says, breathless.

"Of course," Eric says. "I promised I won't leave you."

"Did you bring her too?" Mina asks.

Eric turns. Cassandra is hunched behind him, covered in scaly patches, her eyes bright with fire and pain, about to fall. Eric would catch her, but she holds up a hand, keeps him back.

"I think it's too late for me," she says. "I wasn't strong enough."

"You are," he says to her. "You're the strongest person I know." And then, "This isn't the only way. You don't have to be…this."

Her knees wobble and tears streak across her face. Eric feels closer to Cassanadra now than he ever did when they were physically together. Her voice breaks into a desperate howl. "What else is there?"

Eric had spent so long trying to become one singular thing, a thing he was told he should be. But when he finds himself in the mindscape now, his old body is gone. They—because Eric has almost shed the *he*, shed the *him*, become something different—look different now. But it's not just one body, not really. It's an infinite possibility of them. The Eric they were born as, the Eric they grew up as, and so many more. A version where their wedge-shaped torso tapers into an hourglass instead. One where they are absent nearly all the hair on their body, smooth and beautiful. Another where they ripple with unashamed hairy muscle. Hims and hers and thems and everything in between, a kaleidoscope of possibilities spread out before them, finally unlocked by the color from their meaty jail cell, and it's the most beautiful thing they've ever seen. All they have to do is take that step. All they have to do is be stronger than the fear. Because it's okay for the fear to be there too.

They take Cassandra's hand to show her this. The images flash through the color, lavender to blue, and Eric knows Cassandra is seeing her own version of infinite possibilities because they can feel it too, of her transcending not her body, but her mind. Transcending the mold the world made for her and tried to force her into.

Eric holds out their hands to both Cassandra and Mina. "Do you want to live like this?"

"No," they both say, in their own time.

"Then we'll find another way."

Mina and Cassandra take their hands as, outside the mindscape, the world watches, hushed, confused, as what is supposed to be a frightening battle, a natural disaster, ends not with an explosion, not with screams, not with terror, but with a softness. The three figures at the center of it, the Imago and the Instars, tilt their heads up towards the sky, each pouring forth their colors from every pore, shedding the excess, dropping all the weight they've carried for so long. Before the eyes of the bystanders, the eyes of those watching through military drone cameras, through news clips all over the world, belching color, the running lights on the Instars and the bioluminescence on the Imago going low and then out completely, powering down until they are three people, finally untethered to what they were before, dropping to the street free of their machines, of their shells, riding free on a rainbow wave of colors.

Transcended. Finally loosed from their chains.

ACKNOWLEDGMENTS

The Cosmic Color is the first serious novella I wrote (not counting a bunch of trunk books throughout high school and college), but the second to be published, because everyone's publishing timelines are different. Huge shout-outs have to go of course to dave at Neon Hemlock for believing in this story, editing the absolute hell out of it (seriously, the version you just read is *light years* better than what I submitted), and knowing when it needed just a *little* more work before we put it out in the world. To Vaughn A. Jackson for giving me the first ever book blurb (and one hell of a blurb at that). Thanks to AP Thayer for interviewing me and revealing the absolutely amazing cover, designed by Buttercup (who also did the cover for my debut novella, *The Familialists*). Thank you, Downs, for teaching me about the dust, which I thought about again and again throughout the many versions of this book, and to my partner, for watching endless amounts of anime and *Pacific Rim* on repeat with me while I was getting in the mood to write this.

ABOUT THE AUTHOR

TT Madden (they/them) is a genderfluid, mixed-race author of *The Familialists* who refuses to keep politics out of their books. Their work in scifi, fantasy, and horror often deals with the intersections of their various identities. Their forthcoming novellas include the YA horror *Gorman's House* with Mad Axe Media, and the religious horror *The Neon Revelation* with Timber Ghost Press. They can be found on social media as @ttmaddenwrites.

ABOUT THE PRESS

Neon Hemlock is a Washington, DC-based small press publishing speculative fiction, rad zines, and queer chapbooks. Publishers Weekly once called us "the apex of queer speculative fiction publishing" and we're still beaming. Learn more about us at neonhemlock.com and on social medias at @neonhemlock.

www.ingramcontent.com/pod-product-compliance
Lightning Source LLC
Chambersburg PA
CBHW031344060726
47590CB00007B/2625